D1448570

Also By Fleur Hitchcock

The SHRUNK! Adventures
SHRUNK!
SHRUNK! Mayhem & Meteorites
SHRUNK! Ghosts on Board
SUNK!
and
The Trouble with Mummies
The Yoghurt Plot

FLEUR HITCHCOCK

Piccadilly
PRESS

First published in Great Britain in 2015
by Piccadilly Press
Northburgh House, 10 Northburgh Street, London EC1V 0AT
www.piccadillypress.co.uk

A CIP catalogue record for this book is available from the British Library.

ISBN: 978-1-848-12448-6

1 3 5 7 9 10 8 6 4 2

Printed and bound by Clays Ltd, St Ives Plc

Piccadilly Press is part of the Bonnier Publishing Group
www.bonnierpublishing.com

*For the longshoremen of the Isle of Wight,
both past and present, especially Dad.*

Welcome to
BYWATER-BY-SEA

H

C

B

D

J

A is the model village

B is the castle

C is the school

D is the beach

E is the seawater baths

F is Mr Burdock's donkey field

G is the edge of the village

H is the town hall

I is North Beach and
the nature reserve

J is the pier

Prologue

I was shocked by just how angry the deckchair was.

One minute, we were getting on with a sunny Sunday on the beach. The next, Mr Bissell was racing over the sand, screaming. Apparently pursued by a deckchair.

It's impossible, I know.

But I saw it.

'Dad,' I say on the way home from the beach, laden with buckets and rolly-up things that

1

keep on unrolling. *'Did you notice anything odd?'*

'Odd, Tom? No,' says Dad, swinging a spade onto his shoulder. 'People can get into terrible pickles with deckchairs. So difficult to manage – I never know which bit goes where.'

'Oh,' I say.

But I can't stop thinking about it.

1

What?

Yesterday was the last day of the Easter holidays, and today is the first day of the summer term, so a wet sea squall has blown in and is having a tantrum all over town. I pull my waterproof tight over my chest and thrust my hands deep into my pockets and wait for the school bus at the bus shelter by the model village.

A moment later, Tilly, my younger sister, arrives by my side, and we stand in mutual silence by the road, getting soaked.

'Morning, chaps. Bracing, isn't it?'

Dad?

'What are you doing here?' says Tilly.

'Guess,' says Dad, rubbing his hands together.

Tilly looks disgusted. 'Dunno, I can't imagine.'

Dad smiles smugly and says nothing else.

The bus arrives and we all three climb on. Dad sits at the front with the driver, Tilly joins her friend Milly, and I roll to the back to sit next to Eric.

Eric puts down his copy of *150 Alternative Ways to Spend the Summer Holidays* and looks up. 'Morning, Tom. Why's your dad on the bus?'

I shake my head. I feel about 9% good about the answer to that question.

Eric raises his eyebrows, which means that some pale hairs that are barely visible on his freckly face move closer to some slightly red hairs boinging all over his forehead like broken springs. 'Really?' he says.

I look around. All the usual suspects are there, mostly staring at the lashing rain outside, but some are staring at Dad because no dad ever, ever, ever has, in the history of school buses, caught the school bus. Surely?

Why would my dad be the first?

'Hey, Model Village,' says Jacob from the back seat. 'Daddy coming to school with you today? Is he coming to hold your hand?'

I try to ignore him. 'Did you have a good holiday, Eric?' I ask.

'Yes,' says Eric, looking at me strangely. 'You know I did.'

'Good,' I say. I stare out of the window and I feel a blush start at the bottom of my back and spread up over my face until I'm sure that I'm completely beetroot.

Something appalling has occurred to me. A vision. Something that's been part of our lives all holiday. In my mind's eye I can see the kitchen table, with the *Bywater-by-Sea Gazette* open on page 17 and one advert ringed in red. I've even read it and I know that between the adverts for LOST – ONE TORTOISE and FOUND – ONE TORTOISE is one that says: JOB OFFERED. BYWATER-BY-SEA SCHOOL – REQUIRED: TEACHING ASSISTANT. IMMEDIATE START.

'OH! No!' I mutter.

'What is it?' says Eric.

'It's Dad, he's going to be working at school – every day, all the time.'

'Oh dear,' says Eric. 'Oh dear, Tom. You have my deepest sympathies.'

2

Cold Chips

It takes me until break to remember that I want to tell Eric about yesterday's deckchair-on-the-beach episode. And when I finally find him feeding the Mongolian hawk-moth caterpillars in Mr Bell's classroom, I have walked past Dad handing out juice in the playground three times.

'Hi, Tom,' Dad shouts with enthusiasm. 'Great working here. Lovely to be with you all day.'

All of Year 1 turn and stare as I bolt across the playground.

'How's it going?' asks Eric, tempting a particularly large and repulsive orange caterpillar with a nettle.

'With Dad? Awful,' I say. 'But that's not the point. The point is that something happened on the beach yesterday.'

'Oh?'

'It sounds really silly, but a deckchair attacked Mr Bissell.'

'Attacked how?' Eric puts down the first nettle and picks up a second. They look exactly the same.

I think back to what I saw. 'It folded round him. It sort of pinched him inside.'

Eric drops the second nettle in the tank and turns to face me. 'Fascinating. Just the one?'

'Yes – only one.'

'Did anyone else see?'

Once again I try to remember the scene

exactly as it happened. 'Mum was reading the paper. Dad was building a sandcastle. Mr Bissell's wife must have seen, although she might have been asleep. Oh and Mr Fogg –'

'Albert Fogg – the longshoreman?'

'Yes, him, the one with the beard. The man who hires out the deckchairs and eats crab sandwiches under an umbrella. He must have seen.'

Eric looks wise for a long time before saying, 'Why's your dad taken a job here? I thought he was going to be a magician?'

At lunch, I have to hide behind the bins in the rain.

'Tom, Tom!' Dad's wandering around the playground looking for me. He's wearing a checked pair of trousers, an apron and rubber gloves. 'Tom, love, I thought we could eat lunch together. We could share a bag of crisps.'

'Hiding from Daddy?' says Jacob, rolling round the corner and settling next to the bins. He pulls an enormous greasy package from his pocket.

'What's that?' I ask.

'Yesterday's chips,' he says. 'Want one?'

I shake my head. 'I thought they'd banned chips,' I say.

'They have,' he says. 'That's why I'm round here hiding with a loser like you. No way am I eating salad – so I've brought my own packed lunch.'

He prises a long, soggy, flaccid chip from the pile and dangles it into his mouth. Not only is it cold but it has ketchup embedded between it and the greasy polystyrene box. Jacob's lips close round it and he begins to chew. 'So,' he says. 'Where's Snot Face? Thought you two were always together?'

Snot Face is what Jacob calls Eric. It's unkind, but then Jacob is unkind.

'I'm here,' says Eric. 'And do stop calling me "Snot Face", please, Jacob.'

'As you like, Snot Face,' says Jacob, wiping his mouth with the back of his sleeve.

Eric ignores him. 'So, Tom, what we need is a closer look at that deckchair.'

'What deckchair?' says Jacob.

'The one that attacked Mr Bissell on the beach,' says Eric.

'Sounds exciting,' says Jacob. 'Did it kill him?'

'No,' I say.

'And would it be better if it had?' Eric asks Jacob.

'Yes,' says Jacob.

We both stare at him.

'Was that the wrong thing to say?' says Jacob, polishing off another chip.

'Anyway.' Eric turns back to me. 'Do you think you can get a sample?'

But before I manage to answer, we're interrupted by Dad. 'Tom, darling – there you are. What on earth are you doing here in the rain? Now, boys, come and join me, and I can show you how the potato-peeling machine works. It's absolutely thrilling.'

3

Mum vs Tilly

It almost kills me. The worst bit is when Dad takes the checked trousers off in the middle of the dining room. He has got shorts on underneath but how was I to know that?

At the end of the day, Dad gets on the school bus, whistling, and insists on chatting to everyone. The bus burbles around the town shedding passengers. Dad talks to them as they go.

'Right, Dad,' says Tilly when we finally get off the bus in a howling gale at the bottom of the model village. 'We are going to have some rules.'

'Yes,' I say, for once in total agreement with her.

'Number one,' she says, struggling to put up her pink umbrella. 'You are not allowed on the school bus.'

'Number two,' I say. 'We do not eat lunch with you.'

'Number three,' says Dad. 'You two don't tell me what to do, so put up with it. I've got a job at your school and if you want to eat then that's the way it's going to be.'

'OHHHWWW! Dad!' shouts Tilly. 'That's so unfair!'

'It is, isn't it?' he says, swinging off through the model village whistling.

I stand staring at his back, my heart sinking and sinking. I feel 1% good about this.

'We've got to stop him,' says Tilly. 'This can't go on. I'll die if he asks me one more question about trestle tables. We'll have to have a word with Mum. What are you doing now?'

'Um . . .' I say. 'Going to the beach?'

'Don't be ridiculous, Tom. In this?' She waves her hand through the torrential rain.

So I follow her up to the house.

But Mum's drawing red circles on the newspaper too.

'Shall I train as a plumber?' she asks.

'Very small spaces, dear,' says Grandma, taking a large carving knife to some raisin shortcake and loading it onto inadequately small plates. 'You won't like it.'

'Or an electrician?'

We all stare at Mum. Last time she did anything electrical it was to stick a screwdriver in the top of the washing machine and nearly blow up herself – and the house.

'All right. What about welding? Could I do welding? Or I could be a yoga teacher or learn to make cheese. Or perhaps I should join the –'

'Mum, can you just be quiet?' says Tilly, grabbing a pencil off the table and using it to scratch her head.

Grandma frowns, but Mum turns to Tilly and beams.

'Look,' says Tilly, 'it was bad enough when you and Dad were going to be magicians, but things are much, much worse now.'

'Oh?' says Mum.

'Dad, at school. I'm serious, he is not coming into school again. Ever.'

'Why?' says Mum, reddening.

'Because he's awful – he behaves like . . .

like . . . like a puppy!' shouts Tilly. 'He cannot, I repeat, cannot, come to school again.'

Grandma scowls. Mum folds the paper and opens it again. She doesn't actually look Tilly in the eye. 'NO,' she says. 'He *will* be going to school tomorrow, and the next day. It's his job.'

Tilly looks as if she's going to explode. 'WHAT!!!???'

'And we'd be very grateful if you were actually able to be supportive.'

Tilly doesn't say anything this time but she turns red, then white, then a little green before racing from the room, screaming.

4

Click

I slip out of the back door and through the model village. Mum and Grandma have been working hard. All the hedges are trimmed ready for the summer season and they've laid fresh gravel and cut the grass.

Mum's had loads of time to help Grandma this time because the whole magician thing has gone wrong. We moved here because Mum and Dad wanted to be stage magicians. They gave up perfectly good jobs, a perfectly nice house and some perfectly lovely friends to move here, to be with Grandma, so that we could all live next to the model village. The plan was that they would become stage magicians, tour the country, do the odd cruise, get a telly series, write books and become household names. The reality turned into a free show at the town hall, three children's parties, a sixtieth birthday party, a disastrous ruby wedding anniversary and the disappearing cabinet finale, where they actually disappeared someone. Not even enough to pay for the rabbit food.

Which is why Dad is now working at the school and Mum is looking for another career.

I just hope she's not thinking of working at the school too.

I stumble through the model village, drop down to the Dingly Dell Crazy Golf and clamber over the gnome-covered wall onto the promenade. Huge puddles stretch over the tarmac and under the glass shelters that line the seafront but there's no one hiding inside them. It's simply too wet.

I stop under the amusement-arcade awning and study the beach.

It looks utterly deserted. Out at sea some moored yachts bounce on the waves and in the harbour others jostle and groan against the jetties. A couple of people fight their way along the pier, brollies flipped inside out and coats flapping.

Perfect.

Breaking free of the amusement arcade I dash over the tarmac and race down to the beach steps, water splashing up my trouser legs every step of the way.

Vast heaps of seaweed have been thrown up onto the shore since yesterday and for a moment it looks as if everything has been swept from the beach by the storm, but then I see Albert Fogg, the man who looks after the deckchairs, crouching at the back under an oilskin and a huge umbrella.

Flip.

He's manning the deckchairs. As if on a day like this you'd have to.

I slow down and saunter over the pebbles. A length of seaweed wraps itself round my foot and I spend an unnecessarily long time untangling it, taking the opportunity to have a good look at Mr Fogg.

Normally he wears a navy-blue sweater and the oldest, most faded jeans I've ever seen. His skin is the colour of old crab claws and his eyes are hidden so deeply in the crevasses of his face that I couldn't say if they had a colour at all.

Today he's wearing the full yellow sailor waterproofs and, despite the rain, seems to be washing a deckchair down with a watering can.

Snatches of his song escape through the rain. 'Put him in the scuppers . . .'

He fills the watering can from the beach tap, scuttles back over the shingle and goes at the deckchair with a broom. 'Take that – and that!' he says and then bursts into song again. 'What shall we do with the drunken sailor . . .'

I straighten up and wander past. It's hard to look casual when there's a gale blowing. When I've reached the end of the beach, I shelter under the pier and look back.

I can't work out if this is the deckchair that attacked Mr Bissell. They all look exactly the same, but then why would Mr Fogg single out a lone deckchair for a scrub when he must have a shed full of them?

Above me, the pier whizzes and pings as the unplayed machines try to attract attention. Someone's feet sound on the boards and then thump along to the seafront. The same person pulls their coat close round them and marches along to the set of steps nearest to the beach tap. They trot down the steps, and start to talk to Mr Fogg.

I can't see who it is. They're wearing too many waterproofs. But I can hear some words. 'Not . . . safe . . . secret . . . newspapers . . . not a bean left . . . important . . . vital.'

Mr Fogg nods and pulls his cap.

The wrapped-up person struggles up the steps and into the town, disappearing into the storm.

Mr Fogg opens a door behind him. He places his empty watering can inside and I see a cave that seems to go deep into the solid front of the seafront. He locks the door again and folds the deckchair flat, leaving it lying against the front of the store.

I wait, trying to make myself as thin as one of the pier supports, until he rolls up the steps, along the sea wall and in through the front door of the Trusty Tramper Café.

It's not easy to tiptoe on pebbles, and frankly it's not actually necessary in a gale, but I do tiptoe until I'm over by the deckchair and hidden under the lee of the sea wall.

There's nothing to see. I'm pretty sure it's the same one, as there's a tear in the cloth where I seem to remember Mr Bissell turning and attempting to bite it. Otherwise it looks disappointingly ordinary.

Experimentally I try to lift it. It's quite heavy, but not impossible and I half carry, half drag it along the beach to the very end.

Which is where it gets difficult.

The moment I stick my head over the parapet the wind doubles in strength and seems to change direction so that I'm blown back towards the sea.

'Stupid thing,' I say, pulling it against me. But the wind catches the fabric and tugs both me and the deckchair back down to the beach so that I have to lean the deckchair against the wall and stop to breathe.

Peeling the hood from my face, I let the rain beat on my skin for a minute. This seems ridiculously hard work. Surely it can't be this difficult to move a deckchair?

I lift it again, and again, but I can't quite leave the beach with it.

What?

I make a third attempt, this time with all my strength, but the deckchair becomes heavier than me. I can't actually lift it and when I let go the wind takes it back onto the pebbles.

I stand on the steps, looking down at it.

I'd swear it's got a Tilly face on. Smug.

The rain beats on my head. I am now actually getting wet *inside* my waterproof, and I am officially cross. How on earth am I going to get a sample of this deckchair to Eric?

Back on the beach I check to see if any of the joints are loose. Sadly they aren't.

So I search the tar blobs and fish heads scattered along the beach for something sharp. I find a mussel shell, a biro lid and a piece of slate.

The biro lid bends and the slate shatters but the mussel shell lets me prise the tiniest splinter of wood from the chair, and cuts me a thread of the cloth.

'Ha!' I say to the deckchair. 'Ha! Serves you right.'

The deckchair falls flat on the beach and the splinter and the piece of cloth whisk from my hand and vanish into the wind.

I'd swear that the deckchair laughs.

'OK then. If that's the way you want to play it.'

I hold up my right hand, form an O with my thumb and my forefinger and . . .

Click.

5

Smoothie Volcano

The tiny deckchair is flipping about inside my pocket. I shrank it – it's this thing I can do, but only here in Bywater-by-Sea. If I came round to your house, I wouldn't be able to, and Eric wouldn't be able to produce water from the end of his fingertips and Jacob wouldn't be able to set fire to things.

We've all got strange powers because of the meteorites – the ones from the sky that we caught, and the giant one under the castle. We're not the only ones with strange powers.

Grandma can shrink things too. She knows all about us, but Mum and Dad don't and nor does Eric's dad. It's weird and wonderful, and sometimes gets very complicated.

'Tom, enter.' Eric's dad stands in the doorway. He's wearing pyjama trousers and a parrot-green Hawaiian shirt.

'Hello, Mr Threepwood.'

'Good,' says Eric's dad.

I stand in the hall, not quite knowing what to say. I never know quite what to say with Eric's dad. He's not like other people. But then Eric's not like other people. Most people are not as nice or as clever as Eric or his dad.

'Um,' I say in the end.

Eric's dad smiles and wanders off into the kitchen. I stand for a moment, my hand on the front door, feeling embarrassed.

'Shall I go and find Eric?' I say, but Eric's

dad's not listening. Instead of answering me, he picks up an enormously thick book about space travel and starts eating something that looks very like straw.

Upstairs Eric is playing Scrabble online with someone in Russia. 'That's "keckle" – K-E-C-K-L-E – it means to wind something up with a rope,' he bellows at a tiny picture in the corner of the screen. 'Oh – hello, Tom.'

'I shrank the deckchair and brought it here,' I say, staring at the Scrabble board, which is dotted with words I've never seen before. 'What's a "palpi"?'

A pained expression flickers over Eric's face. 'It's not "a palpi" – palpi are the plural. They're the sensitive bits on a crab – surely you know that, Tom?'

'Anyway,' I say. 'Here it is.' I place the tiny

deckchair on Eric's desk. 'This is *the* deckchair, or at least I think it's *the* deckchair. Albert Fogg was washing it down, and talking to it, when it was big.'

The tiny shrunken deckchair looks like a very careful piece of model-making. It's about the size of my little finger and harmless. In fact, I'd almost call it cute. Eric closes the laptop and peers at the chair. 'Washing it down, you say. Unusual.'

'Will you be able to analyse it? Even if I've shrunk it?'

In answer, he opens a cupboard door. An avalanche of single shoes, game controllers, batteries and last year's cracker presents cascades to the floor. He pushes them out of the way and wades into the debris. 'There should be –' he says, shoving aside a plastic skeleton – 'a microscope here somewhere. I'm sure I saw it . . . Ah!'

Triumphant, he turns, holding a small battered cardboard package and laying it reverently on the desk. It's covered in what looks like Chinese writing and has a picture of a huge spider on the front.

'In here –' he lifts the lid from the box, revealing a brittle plastic insert that's cracked and clings to the object it encloses – 'should be Dad's microscope.' Eric shakes off the shards of once-white plastic packaging and stands a small object on the desk.

'That's a microscope?' I say. It doesn't look anything like the microscopes we use at school.

'It's a bit old – Dad had it when he was a child. 1970s?' He waves the plug at me. 'Put that in over there,' he says, fiddling with what might be the lens.

I plug it in and amazingly nothing goes bang.

'If it isn't a microscope,' says Eric, 'I don't

know what else it could be.' He takes the deckchair from my palm and places it on a dimly lit piece of glass.

I stare, waiting for him to say something, but he doesn't so I sit down and squeeze some water from my trousers.

'Yes,' he says eventually.

'What?' I say.

'This microscope is either not a microscope or it's broken. We'll have to try at school.'

Downstairs, Eric's dad offers me a kelp and hempseed flapjack.

'Er, no thank you, Mr Threepwood,' I say, heading towards the front door.

'Eric?' he says, holding out the plate.

'I'm good, thanks, Dad.'

'Oh.' Eric's dad stares sadly at the plate of misshapen brown things. 'Or a bulgar and wheatgrass smoothie?' He points into the kitchen towards the blender, which seems to have had some kind of green volcanic accident.

I shake my head.

'In that case, take a poster.' He hands Eric the plate and reaches into a wellington boot, pulling out a roll of paper. Striding to the kitchen table, he places a jar of molasses on one end and unrolls the rest.

He peels a sheet from the top and hands it to me. 'Do you think you could put it up in the window of the model village?'

VOTE FOR COLIN THREEPWOOD.

MEDITATION FOR ALL AND FREEDOM

FROM CONSUMER TYRANNY

'Or you could have this one, it's snappier.'

BE POSITIVE. THREEPWOOD FOR MAYOR

I stand staring at the poster. 'Sorry, I don't quite understand. Are *you* running for mayor?' I ask.

Eric's dad nods his head enthusiastically. 'Yes.' He puts his arm round Eric's shoulder. 'I am, totally. Eric, my marvellous son, has persuaded me that I can do it. That I have a lot to offer our community, that I can help lead us into the new millennium with consideration and love and freedom from corporate globality.'

Eric stands by his father's side and beams.

'Right,' I say, rolling up a poster and jamming it under my arm.

'It's all there, Tom. All there for us to take.' Eric's dad stares at me, his eyes big and round. 'Because, Tom, here, at the heart of Avalon, the astral plane is vibrant.'

'Yes, Mr Threepwood,' I say.

'You do understand what that means?'

'Yes, Mr Threepwood,' I say again, wondering what on earth he's on about.

'Anything could happen, Tom.'

I nod vigorously. With enthusiasm.

'It's a wondrous place, this place,' he says.

'Yup,' I say, backing towards the door, clutching my poster. 'Sure is.'

'Tom's got to go now, Dad,' says Eric, opening the door behind me and shoving me out into the street.

'Sure you wouldn't like a flapjack?'

'He wouldn't,' says Eric.

'Pity,' says Eric's dad. 'Pity.'

6

Die, Pasta, Die

Eric's dad running for mayor is unexpected. Although, perhaps it isn't really. Perhaps it's something he'd be brilliant at, but I can't imagine him sitting in a boardroom discussing blocked culverts or parking schemes. He has a weird way of saying things, not like other adults. I don't think most of it means anything, but sometimes some of it means something.

I'm wondering what an astral plane actually is, and about his warning that anything could happen, when I pass a huge stack of newspapers outside the post office.

CHILD EATEN BY HER OWN BUCKET! in the *Bywater-by-Sea Guardian*

WILD CARNIVOROUS PAIL CHEWS CHILD VICTIM in the *Evening Echo*.

And on a copy of the *Bywater Globe*: BRAVE BEVERLEY'S BUCKET FRENZY!

A couple of women are staring open-mouthed at the headlines.

Bucket?

I wonder about nipping back to Eric's but I remember the smoothie volcano and head on round to our house.

Grandma's got the TV on full volume and after we've sat through an item on knitted road signs and another one about novel sandwich fillings, the announcer gets on to Bywater-by-Sea.

'And finally, just at the beginning of the holiday

season, in the sleepy town of Bywater-by-Sea
a young girl had a narrow escape. It's unclear
about the events leading up to the accident, but
it seems that six-year-old Beverley Woodruff of
Bywater Regis was enjoying a wet afternoon on
the beach when she managed to jam a bucket
on her head. At first her parents tried to pull it
off, but then an anxious passer-by called the fire
brigade. Sergeant Bradley Thomas of the local
fire station said, and I quote, "In all the years
I've been a fire officer I've never come across
a more peculiar case. It was as if that bucket
was alive" . . .'

'Well I never,' says Grandma, dropping her
knitting. 'Know anything about this, Tom?'

'No, Grandma.'

She stares at me very hard over her glasses.
'Sure?'

'No – I really don't, honestly.'

* * *

'I'm not eating that,' says Tilly, pushing her plate away.

'But Dad spent hours cooking it,' says Mum.

'Don't care,' says Tilly, scratching her head furiously. 'It's disgusting.'

'Well, I'm not cooking you anything else,' says Dad, doling out the pumpkin pie.

'All right then,' says Tilly, standing up. 'I'll make my own supper.'

'That girl,' mutters Grandma after Tilly has left for the kitchen.

'She's her own worst enemy,' says Mum.

'Bless her,' says Dad.

'Yes,' says Mum. 'It's just a phase. Such a difficult age. Although I wish she could see things from another person's point of view – just sometimes.'

'Complicated girls,' says Dad. 'Not like us, eh, Tom?'

I nod. Tilly is certainly complicated. Whether it's because she's a girl I couldn't say.

There are terrible sounds of pans hitting other pans and things boiling over while Dad, Mum and Grandma scrape their forks on their plates and clear their throats.

'Very nice this pumpkin pie, dear,' says Grandma eventually, chewing hard.

'Lovely,' says Mum, glugging several glasses of water.

I look at the desiccated pumpkin pie lying orangely on my plate. 'Aren't pumpkins things you get in autumn?'

Grandma smiles and pushes a cindery piece of pastry around her plate.

'Just using up the contents of the freezer,' says Dad.

There's a long silence, broken by the sound of Tilly shouting at the fridge.

'Haven't found a job yet,' says Mum.

'How about the ice-cream factory?' says Dad.

'Or the Royal Hotel?' says Grandma. 'I gather they're likely to be under new ownership soon. The dear old Finch sisters have finally given up.'

'I thought I could go into politics,' says Mum.

'Goodness,' says Grandma.

Tilly drops something hard and large into the sink.

'Did you know that Eric's dad is running for mayor?' I ask.

Grandma stops attacking her pastry. 'Colin Threepwood! I don't believe it.'

'Really? How extraordinary,' says Dad, getting up from the table and walking over to shut the door to the kitchen.

Mum sweeps her pie off her plate and into her napkin. 'How interesting,' she says, wandering past the piano and dropping the pie inside. 'I wonder what brought that on.'

I shrug. That's it from me in terms of conversation.

Psshshshshshsh.

A long, rising bubbling sound drifts out from the kitchen and everyone pauses to listen.

'Ah ha!' shouts Tilly. 'Die, pasta, die – you have met your match – I am the queen of all things spaghetti. Melt in my cauldron and quiver . . .'

Briefly I wonder whether the food that Tilly's making might be nicer than Dad's.

Then there's a crackle and a bang and what sounds like a saucepan hitting the kitchen floor.

'Stop it! Stop it! You stupid thing!' shouts Tilly. The back door opens with a crash and the faint whiff of burned pasta floats through into the dining room.

On the other hand . . .

7

Mr Bell's Cardigan

At school, Miss Mawes the art teacher has developed this notion that I'm good at art. I've been avoiding her since term began but just before registration this morning she caught me.

'Tom, at last I've found you. Now, I've got the Sculpture on the Beach details here. You really should enter – you've got a talent.'

This is based on a drawing of a badger that I traced last term for a project. Somehow she thought I'd drawn it from scratch and somehow

I didn't tell her the truth. I shouldn't have done it. I know I shouldn't have done it, but I was desperate and now she thinks I'm Leonardo.

I'd copied it from Eric's *Wildlife Fun for Lively Children* book, which is now hidden under my bed.

'Well, at the very least, come to Art Club. After school, Tuesday. Shall I put you down?'

She took my silence as a yes.

About a foot down the corridor I met Dad, his arms full of cooking ingredients. 'Give me a hand, Tom, just as far as Rainbow Class.'

I debated running away, but left it slightly too long and took the butter and flour from Dad's tottering pile. He pushed the door open with his bum and swung inside. I followed him into the classroom at which point the bag of flour slipped from my hand and exploded on the floor.

There was an awful silence. Someone at the back giggled. Mrs Hawk glared at me. Every single child in the classroom gaped, and some clapped their hands to their mouths dramatically.

'Oh dear,' said Dad.

I turned scarlet and fled.

I'm wondering what I might have done wrong in a former life to deserve Dad, when Eric arrives carrying a copy of the *Bywater Times*. He points at the headline: FIREMEN ACT IN BUCKET MYSTERY.

'Yes,' I say. 'Worrying, isn't it?'

'We need to get this –' Eric uncurls his hand to reveal the tiny deckchair – 'under there.' He points to Mr Bell's pride and joy. The brand-new XX900 Macrocaster, purchased by the PTA with money raised by a sponsored midnight cliff walk. Since the school bought it we've been allowed to look at a fragment of onion skin and the scrapings from under Jacob's nails, which were more lively than expected.

The problem is that the XX900 Macrocaster is behind Mr Bell's desk and takes five minutes to warm up.

'Sooner rather than later,' I say. 'Before it starts to grow big again.'

'So,' says Jacob, appearing behind me. 'What's the plan, team?'

'The plan is –' I say, but I'm interrupted by Mr Bell clapping his hands. I notice he's wearing what can only be described as a cardigan. Which is odd because he normally wears a tracksuit. He's been behaving strangely ever since his wife had a baby.

'Good morning, class,' he shouts, before modulating his voice to something uncharacteristically soft. 'How are we this morning? Are we ready to try a little role play?'

There's a mumble.

'Because – today – we are going to get in touch with our sensitive side. In fact, the whole school is getting in touch with its sensitive side.'

'What?' says Jacob.

Mr Bell sits on the front of his desk and tilts his head towards Jacob in a sympathetic manner. I can't help feeling that he's been practising this in front of the mirror. 'Yes, Jacob. I know that under all that . . . bravado is a sensitive, feeling, human being.'

Mr Bell may be sure, but I'm not.

'Why, Mr Bell?' asks Jacob, scratching his bottom.

'Why what?' asks Mr Bell.

'Why are we getting in touch with our sensitive sides?'

'Very good question,' says Mr Bell, reverting to his normal megaphone volume. 'Does anyone know the answer?'

There's a pencil-rolling silence in which lots of people roll pencils.

'Empathy,' he says in the end. 'We're going to study empathy. So, for starters, I'd like you to look it up, find out what it is and we'll meet again in five minutes with some definitions.'

'"Empathy" and "Mr Bell" are three words that I'd never put in the same sentence,' mutters Eric, reaching for the huge dictionary that he keeps in his bag.

'What's empathy?' says Jacob, taking Eric's sharpener and sharpening his pencil. 'Is it good on toast? Is it necessary? Do I have it?'

'No, yes, no,' says Eric.

I reach for the dictionary. I'm a bit hazy about empathy. It's something Mum says as if it's really important, and which she says Tilly has but keeps hidden.

She never says if I have it.

'It says here,' I say, 'it's the power of entering into another's personality.' I drop my voice to super-quiet. 'How are we going to get to use that microscope?'

'Shape-shifting?' says Jacob.

'No – more like climbing into another person's skin and feeling what they feel from the inside,' says Eric. 'We need a diversion.'

'That's disgusting,' says Jacob, screwing his nose down towards his mouth.

Eric shakes his head and I say, 'Yes, a really good diversion. That keeps Mr B out for at least ten minutes.'

Which is when Jacob's eyes light up as if some kind of electrical impulse has passed through his brain. 'Leave it to me,' he says.

* * *

'Sir, Mr Bell, sir – can I go to the toilet?' Jacob stands with his legs crossed, looking desperate.

'Yes, of course,' says Mr Bell.

Jacob trips out of the classroom.

'So, role play. Now I'd like you to imagine you are someone else in this room. Don't tell us who, we can guess . . .'

Jacob soon trips back into the room, grinning and winking and generally looking as subtle as a thunderstorm.

People are shuffling uncomfortably. 'Sir, can I be you? Is that allowed?'

'I don't want to be anyone else.'

'I don't get this – what does he want?'

'Can *I* go to the toilet, sir?'

'Sir, what's the point of empathy?'

It feels like it could all go horribly wrong. The chatter gets louder and Mr Bell's voice rises to foghorn level just as someone lets out a really long, really high-pitched scream.

'Aaaaaaaaaaarrrrrrghghghghghghghghghgh!'

We all go completely silent and look around.

'There!' shouts the screamer, pointing at Mr Bell's cardigan.

'What?' says Mr Bell.

'Spider,' whispers the screamer.

There's a second's massive silence.

Mr Bell leaps to his feet and jumps and twitches and yells. He rushes out of the classroom still screaming, to yell and jump and run about in the playground, followed by the entire class, laughing and screaming.

'Very effective,' says Eric.

'Quick,' I say. 'The microscope.'

'Good, eh?' Jacob says.

'Yes,' says Eric, pressing a big red button that says 'ON'.

'Can I just ask,' I say, checking from the window that Mr Bell is still writhing in the playground surrounded by our giggling classmates, 'what happened?'

'Well,' says Jacob, reaching into his pocket and finding something covered in fluff, which he then thrusts into his mouth. 'It was that word, "empathy". I thought what it would be like to be Mr B. What it would be like to stand in his shoes. And then I thought: what does Mr B really not like? And then I thought about spiders and then I remembered that there was a particularly large spider in the locker in the PE store. So I went to get it. Empathy, see?'

'It's not really what empathy means,' says Eric, peering through the lens on the now humming XX900 Macrocaster.

'But you said you had to imagine being someone else.' Jacob sounds puzzled.

'You do – but not usually like that,' I say.

'Oh,' says Jacob. 'So scaring Mr B wasn't empathy?'

By the microscope Eric lets out a long loud sigh.

'It'll help us find out what's wrong with the deckchair,' I say.

'So on balance, it's probably OK?'

I nod. Eric shakes his head.

'Good,' says Jacob. 'Good.'

8

Like a Zombie

'So what did you find?' I ask Eric on the bus home.

Eric puts his copy of *Maths Daily* back into his satchel. 'Well – I had such a short time to look, but there was definitely something wrong with it. The cell structure had changed.'

'Not just because I shrank it?' I ask.

Eric shakes his head. 'No, the cells were smaller – but they were also . . . alive?'

'How do you mean "alive"?'

Eric shrugs and stares out of the window until I wonder if he's forgotten that we're actually having a conversation. 'It seems fanciful, but alive, like animal cells. Not like plant cells,' he says eventually.

'What?'

'I know.'

'But that's terrifying.'

'Yes,' says Eric. 'It is. Oh look, here comes your dad.'

Dad climbs onto the bus and immediately starts singing 'Ten Green Bottles'. I shrink into my seat and watch the steam rise from the top of Tilly's head.

'*And if ten green* – join in, everyone – *bottles should . . .*'

Jacob bellows the words along with Dad and most people join in, in a humming embarrassedly sort of a way.

'C'mon, Tom, you can sing too – *should accidently fall* . . . Oh and I've booked us in for parents' night.'

I acknowledge him with a panicky squeak.

'So both of us can come. I said I'd do the refreshments – *nine green bottles* . . .'

Tilly turns to glare at Dad. Her face is mostly white with two angry pink circles under her eyes.

I reposition myself so that I can't actually see any members of my family. 'So, Eric, are you saying that the deckchair is a living being?'

Eric, who has completed all twenty-seven of the sudokus in *Maths Daily* in the time it's taken Dad to reach two green bottles, closes his eyes for a moment. 'I wouldn't like to say "living". I'm not sure it's really sentient.'

'Are you saying the deckchair is like a zombie?'

Eric nods. 'Yes, very like a zombie. And like a zombie that is activated by the sand or seawater or something frequently occurring on the Bywater beach.'

'Good,' I say, horrified by the words I'm saying. 'So, to sum up, we have a case of a zombie deckchair and possibly a zombie bucket, zombified by something plentiful and naturally occurring.'

'Yes,' says Eric cheerfully. 'That about states the case.'

'What did you do with the deckchair?'

'It's here. Do you want it?' says Eric, digging it out of his satchel and handing it to me.

It's already larger than it was when I gave it to Eric. And it seems to be moving slowly, lugging itself around my palm. Like a zombie.

I listen to Dad chanting '*One green bottle . . .*' and stare at the rain beating down on the pavement outside and the steam filling up the windows of the bus. I turn the deckchair over and over in my hand and wonder just how to deal with a collection of zombified seaside equipment.

9

But, Mum, you CAN'T

At the model village bus stop I jump from the bus to a dry paving slab, which tips and shoots water up the back of my trouser leg.

'Bye, all,' shouts Dad, skipping down the step and tripping along the pavement.

Tilly gets off too and, head bent against the rain, walks dismally behind him. She looks completely furious.

I wait a decent time and follow. I'm not sure what to do with the deckchair that Eric gave me, so I'm thinking of leaving it in the model village. If it's really a zombie then presumably at some point it will take off and march back to the beach. If it isn't, it will grow back to normal size and look like someone left it there for a prank. Either way, I don't want it in my bedroom.

I place it by the tiny cricket match. It looks utterly harmless. Perhaps Eric's completely wrong about this. Perhaps it was some kind of freak wind and he's been looking through the wrong end of the microscope.

I head back up towards home, pulling my hood close around my head, but I'm brought up short by the village noticeboard.

On one side, a handmade rain-smudged politely placed poster, barely covering anyone else's adverts: IF YOU LIKE DECENCY AND WHOLEFOODS – VOTE FOR COLIN THREEPWOOD. On the other, a dayglo-orange big-print banner: SARAH PERKS FOR MAYOR.

Sarah Perks? That's Mum's name.

A horrible sense of misgiving slides over me. My percentage of happiness sinks from 61 to 0.

'She wouldn't,' I say to one of the Dingly Dell elves on the wall of the crazy golf course.

The elf drips back at me, a horrible fibreglass grin stretched across its face.

'But, Mum, you CAN'T.' Tilly's voice greets me before I even reach the front door. 'I'll never live it down.'

'It's not a question of you, Tilly. Or even me. It's a question of what's good for the community.'

Mum's sitting at the kitchen table with a stack of dayglo posters and a huge pen, writing our telephone number on them all. 'And I will be good for the community. I intend to wipe out all corruption and run on a ticket of transparency.'

'Community? Transparency? What about me?' Tilly grabs my arm. 'Us?'

I pull back. I don't like being caught up in Tilly's arguments. They can be very unstraightforward.

'Don't be silly, Tilly. You'll survive.' A slight look of panic comes into Mum's eyes and she speaks a little too loudly. I can see that Tilly's got her worried so she does what I do with Tilly – avoid making eye contact. 'And actually I can't just be a stay-at-home mum to please you. I've a life to live too you know. I'd like a little excitement before it's too late.' She finishes the telephone numbers and reaches for a stack of envelopes and a pile of stickered addresses. 'Quite frankly, I'd like to see the bright lights once in a while. So put up with it.'

Grandma crangs down the lid of the Aga and crashes about with saucepans. It kind of fills the gap but there's still a huge silence in the room.

'Do you fancy a rice pudding this evening, Sarah?' says Grandma.

'Good idea,' says Mum, building up a rhythm with the stickers and envelopes. Mum's new career in politics doesn't look very exciting to me.

I glance over at Tilly. It's as if someone has sucked all the air out of her. Her shoulders are bent and her whole body droops. She scratches her head and pulls her hair down so that it hangs over her face. She draws in a long breath, but instead of speaking she lets it out in tiny bursts of almost sobbing, finished with a loud rattling sniff.

I wait.

She breathes in and out again, and the almost sobbing becomes louder and more definite, followed by another sniff. 'But, Mum,' she says in a near whisper, 'it's child cruelty.' I risk eye contact and notice that her eyes have changed from narrowed and angry to big and pathetic. She stops, waiting for the effect her words will have.

Mum goes on sticking stickers on envelopes. Grandma thumps a bag of sugar on the table.

Tilly sighs, and with a beautifully stifled sob goes on: 'You'll be ignoring us, following a career in politics while your children go unshod and unfed, languishing and forgotten.' She rubs her nose with the back of her hand before scratching her head violently.

'Oh stuff,' says Grandma, pulling out a pudding basin. 'I've never heard such nonsense.'

Tilly heaves a huge sigh, the biggest yet. I can actually see a tear dribbling down her cheek.

'I'll go up to my cold room then, and read a book, and wait until supper time. Don't worry too much about a pudding – I don't think I'll be able to eat one – I'm so . . . unhappy.'

She's wasted as a child. She should be an actress.

10

Pineapple Soup

That sand-dribbling thing is all very well but it gets boring after an hour or two.

It's Saturday. The day of the Sculpture on the Beach contest. It was Eric's idea, and Mrs Mawes's and Mum's and Dad's actually, but at no point was it my idea that I should enter. I don't like sculpture, I don't know anything about art, and I don't much like beaches. Except when they're empty or with jet skis or something. Not Bywater-by-Sea's skanky dead-starfish beach, with sunburned families in too-small bathing suits and REAL ARTISTS.

There's this tall skinny couple hopping around with seaweed that they're draping over a broken piece of fibreglass boat. 'Reminds one of Hockney, don't you think, Orlando?'

'You're so right, Sappho. It's etiolated, and so in the now, of the moment. Genius.'

To me, it looks very much like a piece of yellow fibreglass with a blob of seaweed. I turn back to my creation. So far I've moved a lot of sand from one place to another and found a toothpaste-tube lid and the head of a Barbie doll.

Eric is, in theory, helping me. In fact, he's watching everyone with his binoculars and taking notes. He's doing it from underneath a sheet of black nylon. 'It's a fact: black is better at keeping out the UV rays, Tom.' But I notice that the tiny corner of his elbow that sticks out is already turning red. I move my beach umbrella so that it covers him better.

I can see that everyone else on the beach had an idea before they arrived. In my case it was last minute. Like, eight o'clock this morning last minute.

'So what I'm thinking,' said Eric, 'is that I'll help you do the Sculpture on the Beach contest and that way keep an eye on things. We can both be on duty as it were.' Which is why we're here, unprepared, with a bunch of arty people who actually want to do it.

I knock the top from my sand dribbling and flatten the site. Even though there's only an hour left, sometimes things just have to start again.

'How's Leonardo getting on?' asks Jacob, appearing behind me, ice cream in hand. 'Want any help?'

I look up in surprise.

'I'm doing that empathy thing,' he says, taking a large lick from his ice cream, which is already flowing freely over his hand. 'I imagined that what my mum wanted was some soup, so I made her some.'

Eric pulls the black sheet from his head and stares. 'You made your mum some soup?'

Jacob nods happily. 'Yes. I got a load of stuff from the fridge, stuck it through the blender and boiled it up.'

'What sort of stuff?' I ask, plunging my spade into the sand, and digging a ring around a central pile.

'Oh, you know – onions and pineapple and bacon and yoghurt and stuff she likes. She was so pleased she sent me off with the money to buy myself an ice cream.'

'Wow,' says Eric, pulling the sheet back over

his head. 'Wow, wow and double wow.'

'So I'm wondering if I can help you now, Tom?'

Jacob's feet sink slightly into the sand and his ice cream drips on my trench. I'd really like to send him away but I know, because Eric has told me, that if Jacob is ever to become a better person he needs to understand how much pleasure being nice can give to everyone.

'Well,' I say, 'you could dig this ring for me. I was thinking of something . . . striking. Something modern.'

The skinny couple along the beach catch the word 'modern' and nod at each other and rub imaginary beards.

Jacob digs with enthusiasm, much like a dog, scattering sandy blobs over me and Eric and his sheet and even towards the arty couple. 'So what are you doing, Snot Face? Turning red?'

'I'm watching out,' whispers Eric.

'For what?'

'More anomalies,' says Eric.

Jacob looks confused.

'More things like the violent deckchair and crazed bucket,' I say. 'He's being a kind of lifeguard.'

The light of understanding comes on behind Jacob's eyes.

And we dig.

'Five minutes,' calls the man with the megaphone. 'Five minutes to finish your creations.'

Eric wakes up under his sheet. 'What? Has anything happened?'

'No,' I say. 'What shall we do with this? Suggestions – quick.'

We stare at our construction. It's a mound. Not round, not square, not rectangular, just a mound. Like a termite nest or a pile of gravel. I look across the beach. Stretching away towards the sea are dozens of beautifully arranged castles, sand people, shells and creatures made of driftwood, all obviously made by people with more than a gram of art in their bodies. People for whom artistic achievement means more than tracing a badger from a book.

I look back at the mound and feel about 13% good. It's not that I want to be good at art. I just don't want to be laughed at.

'Can we do anything?' asks Eric, staring across the acres of other people's efforts.

'I could trash all the others?' says Jacob helpfully.

We ignore him.

Beyond the arty couple, a family have built an enormous sand house with gardens and plants and bridges and tiny people made of driftwood. For a moment I wonder if I should just shrink something to put on the mound. Something that would be unbelievably cute and win us the prize, and then I remember that that would be wrong. I stuff my hands in my pockets and, along with the toothpaste-tube lid, I find Barbie's head. Pulling it out, I yank her sandy knotted nylon hair straight and jam her in the top of the mound.

'There,' I say.

'What? That's it?' asks Jacob.

'Yup,' I say. 'Where's the entry form, Eric?'

Eric pulls a crumpled piece of paper from his pocket and hands me a pen.

Buried, I write. And then I put my name and address and skewer it with a seagull feather to the sand.

'Done,' I say, wiping the sand from my hands on my shorts.

Which is when it all kicks off.

11

A Gust of Wind

People run fast when they're scared.

Two children come first, dodging the artworks, racing over the shingle, followed by their pink and flustered mother.

'Is this it?' says Eric, peering past with his binoculars. 'I can't see anything.'

'That's because you're looking the wrong way,' says Jacob. 'Flippin' heck!'

I turn to see what Jacob's looking at.

Three angry deckchairs are stumbling over the sand, mashing the sculptures and sending people running. Alongside them, a small parasol charges at a man and smacks him on his backside. It tires of hitting him and moves on quickly to a woman and does the same to her.

'Oh no,' I say, watching the beautiful sand house mangled by a furious windbreak. It dances and stamps and thwacks until the house lies pulverised, then it paces over to a carefully constructed miniature helter-skelter and dashes it to the ground. Briefly occupied by the destruction of the remaining fairground it's wrestled to the ground by a family and trussed with a yellow bikini. The deckchairs, on the other hand, are now encircling a group of screaming toddlers, slowing down and looking altogether more menacing.

'What are we going to do?' asks Eric, looking as if he'd quite like to run from the beach too.

'We're goin' to mash 'em,' says Jacob, struggling to his feet.

'With what?' shouts Eric at Jacob's back.

But Jacob doesn't hear. He's charging directly at the deckchairs. I catch up easily and try to get a sight on them, but I can't shrink the deckchairs without shrinking the children. 'Jacob!' I shout. 'Be careful, the children.'

'Help!' From behind us comes a voice that sounds awfully like Eric's. 'Tom! Jacob!'

My legs keep running but I turn my top half. Eric's pinned to the ground by a deckchair. All I can see are arms and legs. 'I'll be back in a second,' I shout to him, almost overtaking Jacob.

A flash of fire leaps from the ends of Jacob's fingers – I don't think anyone else sees; I think they're too busy running from the chairs – and strikes the nearest deckchair. It twists, and if a deckchair can glare, it glares at Jacob. As if they could communicate with each other, the deckchairs leave the toddlers and form a line in front of us.

I raise my hand – this time I can shrink them. I form an O with my thumb and forefinger.

Click.

At exactly the same moment Jacob unleashes a cloud of sparks that shower the chairs. I look into my hand immediately after the shrinking to find a collection of tiny writhing burning things while around us the beach falls suddenly calm, filled with nothing more than a puff of smoke and some confused people.

'HELP!' comes a strangled cry. I stuff the chairs in my pocket and we reach Eric at the same time as Albert Fogg, who grabs the chair and wrenches it off Eric's chest. It takes all four of us to pin it to the ground and it doesn't go down easily, snapping its wooden jaws and trapping our fingers.

'Ow!' says Jacob, his eyes flashing red as he emits a random cloud of sparks.

'Jacob,' I hiss. 'Don't, not here.'

We stand on the four corners of the chair while it squirms beneath our feet.

'Well,' says Albert Fogg, taking his battered blue hat from his battered brown head and wiping his brow. 'That was one hell of a gust of wind.'

'Wind?' says Jacob. 'Wind?!'

'You can get some shocking squalls along here – fair take your breath away – and those deckchairs present a big face to the wind.'

Beneath our feet, the deckchair quivers. Mr Fogg leans over and slips a leather belt round the wooden structure and tips it on its side. 'Anyway, thanks, lads,' he says, and he wanders off along the beach dragging the chair behind him.

I reach into my pocket to have a look at the tiny singed chairs. They're lying flat, folded and peaceful.

'Have you got a crisp packet or something, Jacob?' I ask. 'For these.'

Jacob searches his pockets while Eric stares at my catch. Jacob hands me an empty bag of Super Cheese Crunch Puffs and I pop the deckchairs inside.

We sit back on the sand next to our mound, which has survived intact. Even Barbie's hair is untroubled.

The arty couple next to us return and fiddle with their fibreglass, which was flattened by the deckchair furore, arranging it completely differently but looking quite pleased with the result.

We sit in silence, staring, thinking, listening.

'Gosh, what a shock that wind was,' says a woman.

'A gale – all of a sudden,' replies her husband.

'I'd call that a storm,' says another.

'Always thought this was such a sheltered place – perhaps we should try Bywater Regis next time, they do jet skis there too.'

'Oh yes, Bywater Regis is very nice. Faces south too.'

Some people pack up their things and leave the beach. Others rebuild their sculptures and sit nervously staring out to sea.

'There's no way that was a gust of wind,' I say in the end.

'No, well, we know it wasn't, because of old clever clogs here,' says Jacob.

'Yes,' I say, 'but what I'm saying is that Mr Fogg can't possibly think it was either. He's already had three incidents on the beach. He must have seen them all.'

'Hmmm,' says Eric. 'Perhaps we need to talk to him – subtly, you know.'

And then the ice-cream van arrives.

12

An Extra-large, Double Chocolate Golden Syrup Sponge Ninety-nine, Please

De-ding-de-ding-ding.

'Free ice cream for everyone! Come and get it!' blares the horn on the top of the van.

'Really?' says Jacob, springing to his feet.

We wander over to see what's happening. The mayor is inside the ice-cream van handing out lollies and cornets. Beside him, Albert Fogg is sweating and smiling and looking nervous.

'Roll up, roll up,' says Mr Fogg. 'Get your

free ice cream, best ice cream in the Bywater area – far better than Bywater Regis.'

Some of the families who had packed up to leave the beach trail back and loiter by the van.

'Can I have one, Mum?' says a little girl.

'They'll be free all day,' says the mayor, handing down a cone dotted with sprinkles and raspberry sauce. 'To make up for the wind.'

'Oh, I suppose so,' says the mother. 'I'll have one too.' She drops the beach rugs on the ground and takes an ice cream from the mayor, licking chocolate sauce from her fingers.

Jacob takes an extra-large, double chocolate golden syrup sponge ninety-nine and eats it in two bites.

Eric and I sit on the sea wall. Jacob joins us and we all have to move up to make room for his massive bottom.

'No chance of talking to Albert Fogg now,' says Eric. 'Far too public.'

We sit in silence, listening to seagulls and watching families slowly returning to the beach.

'It's both of them, isn't it?' I say eventually.

'The mayor too?' asks Eric.

'Yup,' I reply, taking out the crisp packet and staring in at the three deckchairs. 'They wouldn't make all this effort if they believed the wind story.'

'So why are they covering up?' he asks.

I wave my arm to show all the families on the beach and the others wandering up and down the promenade. 'Because of business,' I say. 'If Bywater-by-Sea gets a reputation for crazed deckchairs the families won't come. They won't go to the cafés or stay in the hotels or buy things from the shops. Even the model village will lose out.'

'Oh,' says Eric, obviously thinking about money for the first time in his life. 'I get it. But . . .' He furrows his brow. 'If they let it go on like this, someone's going to get seriously hurt.'

'They're going to need a bigger ice-cream van,' says Jacob, licking his lips.

'Exactly,' I say.

Much to my surprise, Mum hands me a box of jelly fruits when I get home.

'You won Sculpture on the Beach,' she says. 'I knew you were arty. I can see it now: your first exhibition at the Tate. I've got your whole career mapped out.'

'How?' I say. 'Most of the sculptures got mashed by . . . the wind. There can't have been many left to judge.'

'Gimme,' says Tilly, marching into the kitchen and spying my jelly fruits. 'I'll have those.'

'But you don't even like jelly fruits,' I say, clutching them to my chest.

'Nor do you,' she says.

'But they're mine,' I say.

'And they left this comment about your work,' says Mum, ignoring Tilly. 'Where is it? Oh yes. *A timeless modernist piece, so witty and enlightening. The juxtaposition of consumerist society with the earthy fundamentalism of the sand made a profound commentary. Bravo.*'

'What does that mean?' I ask, still clutching my jelly fruits.

She reads it again. 'No idea,' she says. 'But it means you're doing Art Club.'

'He can't do Art Club,' says Tilly. 'I do Art Club and I don't want him there.'

I didn't want her at Field Craft, but she came – though I don't think I actually said anything to Mum.

Mum pulls a tight smile and faces Tilly. She doesn't even say anything.

Tilly stares. Her face crumples and spouting tears she runs from the kitchen. 'Nobody loves me,' she wails, racing up the stairs and slamming her bedroom door.

In my room I empty the three miniature deckchairs out of the bag and examine them. They're really cute. So cute I'd love to show them to Tilly, because I actually feel quite sorry for her. Never in her whole life have people stood up to her, but now, for the first time, Mum is taking a stand. I've always felt very alone in my wars with Tilly. She seemed to be able to bend Mum and Dad round her little finger and it must be a shock for it to end.

Actually, perhaps I don't feel that sorry.

I look around for something really secure for the deckchairs and dig out a tin of pirates. Emptying the pirates on the floor I jam the deckchairs in and the lid on and then tie my belt round it. I'll be fine as long as I remember to check them regularly.

I open the pack of jelly fruits and stick one in my mouth. It's not very nice and I'm chewing and swallowing just as Tilly appears in the doorway, no sign of tears any more. She sticks her hand out. 'Can I have one?' she demands.

'Say please,' I say.

'Please may I have one?' she says, her voice filled with sugar.

I hold the box out.

'Which one's your favourite?' she asks.

I look. They're all disgusting but probably the blackcurrant. I point at a purple sweet.

'Right,' she says, picking it from the box, sticking it in her mouth and then almost immediately spitting it out of the window.

'What did you do that for?' I ask. 'That was the only one I liked.'

'Exactly,' says Tilly, leaving the room.

I don't feel even a little scrap sorry for her any more.

13

Potato Clock

On the TV news, they say wind.

There's a blurry video of the deckchairs near the toddlers with shouting and juddering camera angles. The newscaster is talking over the top of the pictures: '. . . *shocking holidaymakers and surprising Albert Fogg, longshoreman . . .*' There's a shot of Albert Fogg looking hot and bothered. '. . . *and how did it end? This is from eyewitness reports. It seems that the deckchairs blew into a handily placed beach barbecue because they, and I quote, "appeared to vanish in a cloud of sparks".'*

Grandma raises her eyebrow and continues to knit. She's making what appears to be a church cosy for the model village – made of recycled plastic string from the beach. 'Anything to do with you, Tom?'

I shake my head. I could tell her, but then I'd have to say I shrank the deckchairs in full view of hundreds of holidaymakers and that wouldn't go down at all well.

Next, after a brief history of the town, the camera settles on the mayor. He's also looking hot and bothered. The interviewer sticks a microphone under his nose. 'What do you make of today's events?'

The mayor beams into the camera lens. 'It's just a storm in a teacup so to speak.' He smiles again. 'Nothing to alarm anyone, no harm done, nothing more than a freak wind at the wrong time of year and, for those who do decide to holiday in Bywater-by-Sea, there's free ice cream – yum yum.'

'So the free ice cream doesn't have anything to do with your forthcoming mayoral election?'

'No,' says the mayor. 'Not at all.'

'It does,' says a familiar voice off camera. 'It has everything to do with it. Admit it – you're buying them.'

Oh no. Mum.

The camera swings to Mum's face. She's holding Tilly's hand very tightly as it happens.

'And you are . . .?' asks the interviewer.

Mum kicks Tilly and a snarling Tilly holds up one of Mum's posters, showing it for a nanosecond before the camera judders off to one side. 'Yes – I'm Sarah Perks, running on a ticket of transparency . . .'

The interviewer makes embarrassed throat-scraping sounds. So does the mayor and the camera swings round to the beach again, which looks peaceful and empty.

'Gosh,' says Grandma, switching over to the wrestling.

'Tom,' says Dad, appearing beside me. 'Bored?'

'Not really,' I say. 'I've got one or two things – pieces of homework – in my bedroom,' I lie.

'Oh, they won't take you long. I thought you might like to make a potato clock with me,' says Dad.

'Seriously?' I ask.

But Dad trundles off into the kitchen anyway. 'Can we try a potato and a grapefruit?' he shouts to no one in particular. 'I just want to see if it works before I show it to the littlies.'

14

Best Sunday EVER

On Sunday, nothing happens.

Nothing on the beach or at home.

Nothing, unless you count Tilly going into high-velocity sulk mode.

She doesn't eat.

Doesn't sing.

Doesn't laugh.

Doesn't speak.

Doesn't cry.

It's great. Lovely. The best Sunday EVER!

15

No One Calls a Teacher by their First Name

Monday tries to make up for it.

'Parents' night tonight,' says Dad, picking up a purple-spotted backpack and slinging it over his shoulder.

'You're not wearing that, are you?' I ask.

'I thought I'd get down with the kids – like hip with the groove, YO?' says Dad, doing something only people under fifteen should do with their hands.

Tilly flatly refuses to catch the bus.

'But you have to go to school,' says Mum.

Tilly crosses her arms and purses her mouth into a fine pout.

'You'll have to walk,' says Grandma.

In the end, Mum drives her, while I sit on the bus with Dad thinking dark thoughts, especially about parents' evening.

'I could *not* come,' I say to Eric. 'I could let them come in on their own. Wander about, embarrass Tilly, and I could be at home.'

'My dad'll come,' says Eric. 'I can't imagine your parents will be worse than that.'

But they are. Much worse.

First, we arrive early. Mum and Dad sit on the row of tiny chairs that have been placed in the middle of the hall and wait like expectant cartoon rabbits, smiling and keen and awful. Dad's so tall his knees are up by his chin.

I sit at the other end of the row, pretending to be unrelated. Tilly has hidden in the toilets. I suspect she might have to spend the whole evening there.

'Hello, Mr and Mrs Perks. Hello, Tom,' says Mrs Mawes, sitting at her table on the side. 'Well done for winning Sculpture on the Beach. Top work.'

I blush.

'He's so clever,' says Mum. 'They said it made a *profound commentary*.'

Mrs Mawes gives me a patronising smile.

'Oh, and can I give you one of these?' says Mum, brandishing a dayglo flyer with SARAH PERKS FOR MAYOR printed on it.

'Oh.' Mrs Mawes looks surprised. 'Thank you.'

As she stuffs it under her desk, Eric and his dad stroll in.

'Er, um, Mrs Mawes?' says Eric's dad. 'Can I give you one of these?' He hands her a badly photocopied sheet with SMALL IS GENERALLY NICER scrawled on it in different coloured felt-tips.

Mrs Mawes reddens and puts it under her desk with mum's flyer.

I hope there aren't any other parents running for mayor.

Other teachers arrive and the hall begins to hum with activity. Parents flow in and out, including Jacob's, who manage to look more embarrassed than most of the kids.

Dad makes tea for people and rattles around the hall with a trolley and an apron. I stare at the floor and try to imagine myself somewhere else – like on the beach, in the sunshine, without any deckchairs.

'Mind out, Tom. Stop daydreaming – you

could help me with these.' Mum springs up and hands out more of her flyers. Eric's dad also hands out flyers but he's more polite and less aggressive. Eric doesn't seem to mind, but I just want to sink through a hole in the ground.

'So the thing is,' says Mum loudly to Emily Smee's mum. 'I'm thinking honesty, transparency, no more corruption, and this whole beach thing – it's definitely a cover-up.'

Eric's head snaps up, so does mine.

'Oh?' says Emily Smee's mum. 'Covering up what?'

'I don't exactly know,' says Mum. 'I'd love to get to the bottom of it – I mean, free ice cream? And wind? Could wind really cause all that rumpus?'

'Agreed,' says Sanjeev's dad from behind us. 'It makes no sense.'

'It's the veil,' says Eric's dad. 'Too thin here. Things happen.'

'Funny things do happen,' says Dad, parking his trolley next to us and sitting down. 'Remember that hole in our roof? I've always thought that was very odd, and that thing that happened to Tilly's birthday cake.'

'Oh yes,' says Mum. 'And all the ghostly things that happened before they built the theme park.'

'And the mining in the castle with all the strange lights –'

'Dad,' I interrupt. 'I think it's our turn.'

I practically shove my parents towards Mr Bell's desk, which is far too small for him. There's some jostling while we all cram around it, feeling uncomfortable and generally being too big.

'Tom,' says Mr Bell, holding his fingers together in a considered and intelligent way. 'Tom, Tom, Tom. Lovely Tom.'

I can see by the cardigan and cravat that Mr Bell is still in his 'sensitive' phase.

'Tom.' He breathes in slowly and exhales noisily. I wonder if for some awful moment he's forgotten who I am.

There's a long hideous silence in which we hear all the other parents and teachers chatting away.

'Marvellous,' he says in the end. 'Marvellous.'

'So glad, Graham,' says Dad.

Graham?!?

No one calls a teacher by their first name. That is simply forbidden. Isn't it?

Mr Bell smiles back at Dad. I'm not sure he smiles with his eyes though.

'So.' Mr Bell shuffles through the notes on the table. 'This term we've been doing empathy . . .' Mum makes approving noises. 'I think it's very important,' says Mr Bell, doing the hands thing again. 'It's part of making a strong community.'

'Absolutely, Graham, couldn't agree more,' says Dad, puppy-like.

'Yes,' says Mr Bell, looking confused.

I notice Tilly fiddling with the overhead projector nearby.

'So what should we be doing to encourage empathy in Tom?' asks Mum.

A picture of Mum and Dad's *Alice in Wonderland*-themed wedding comes on the screen. Dad dressed as the white rabbit, Mum as the dormouse. One person giggles.

'Well,' says Mr Bell, 'I don't know. Empathy is of course important, but so is art – and, er – physics.'

Next, a baby picture of Dad dribbling, followed by a shot of Mum aged two, sitting naked on a bucket.

Another giggle.

'I'm concerned that Tom may be wasting what is obviously a very important talent.'

A silent film of Mum dancing in an overly tight golden-sequinned body stocking cuts quickly to a video. There's sound too.

This time everyone stares at the screen. It's been filmed in the bathroom really recently. I can tell because most of Dad's hair has gone. The camera seems to be in the mirror. He's facing it and first he blows himself a kiss.

Everyone in the hall laughs. Except Mum and Dad.

Next, he practises the 'yo' hands. Doing things with fingers splayed in a V, and shuffling his shoulders. He does jazz hands at the mirror, and sings loudly. Then he tries to rap.

I bury my face in my hands, and a huge roar goes up. I have to know what's going on so I peer between my fingers to see the screen cut to another video, this one downloaded from the Internet. It's Mum, microphone in hand, singing: 'I'm walking on sunshine – ooh – oooooooh . . .' It's flat. It's awful. It's the Christmas karaoke that they did in the privacy of the sitting room. Tilly must have filmed it.

It goes on.

Two seconds of Mum practising Spanish verbs.

Three seconds of Dad swearing at a flat tyre.

A shot of Dad's favourite tracks on his iPod. They're all terrible.

I stare at Tilly. She's got the biggest smile on her face.

A photo of Mum's giant purple running pants.

A picture of Dad wearing the chef's trousers in the playground at school.

And finally a photo of Dad aged about seven, standing on stage dressed as a donkey.

I die.

16

Walking on Sunshine

'I don't know how you could do such a thing,' barks Mum, marching Tilly back to the car.

Tilly doesn't speak. She can't wipe the smile off her face and I'm wondering whether when I kill her, I'll bother to hide the evidence.

She scratches her head and turns to stare out of the window, but I can still see the reflection of her smile.

We drive home in silence and, suitably, it begins to rain, driving a fine sea mist over the windscreen and merging low cloud with the oncoming night.

I lie awake for hours that night thinking dark thoughts about Tilly, deckchairs, parasols, Mr Fogg and then even darker thoughts about Tilly.

I sleep badly, waiting for the awfulness of morning. On balance I'd rather deal with violent deckchairs than public humiliation.

'So – Mumsy-wumsy's a singer, is she, Tom?' says Jacob before I've even taken my place on the bus.

I stare rigidly through the window.

'And Daddy too,' he says, and then he breaks into song: 'I'm walking ooooooooon sunshshshshshineeeee – ooooooh – ooohhhh ...'

Belt up, Jacob, I think. But I don't say anything.

Dad's quiet this morning too.

Tilly's talking in a loud voice to her friend, Milly. 'Well, I thought why should I have to suffer? It's their fault, they can suffer.'

'But it's not really Tom's fault,' says Milly. 'And it must be horrible for him.'

For the first time ever I feel something vaguely warm towards Tilly's best friend.

Eric glances over the top of *Extra Physics for Lively Youngsters*. 'Sorry, Tom,' he says. 'It was funny though.'

I don't reply. I feel completely betrayed.

It gets worse.

'Had a good time in the bathroom, Mr Perks?' says someone.

'Are we going to have a singing mayor?' asks another.

Mr Bell doesn't mention it all the way

through ICT, until we get to the very end.

'So, as Tom's parents' illustrated so well last night, we do all need to be very careful what we put on the Internet. It can come back to haunt us.' He beams at me and I try really hard not to run out of the room screaming.

I walk home, which takes ages, and Eric walks with me because he's essentially empathetic.

Jacob comes too. He's not empathetic. He's curious and he can't resist bringing up last night's humiliation at every turn.

'*Walking on sunshine . . . oo-ooooh!* How does it go, Tom?' says Jacob. 'What's the next bit?'

The rain is slightly less than torrential and slightly more than drizzle.

'Yo – Tom,' Jacob says. 'Yo! LOL – yo! Or is it both bits at once? Like . . . YOLO! Isn't that what your dad says?'

We splat through puddles and around the ancient overflowing gutters and drains of the town.

'So, Model Village, how does it feel to have such idiots as parents?'

'Don't,' says Eric quietly behind me.

'Why not?' says Jacob.

'Because it's unkind,' says Eric.

'Oh!' says Jacob. As if he's surprised by the news.

I'm so obsessed by the whole Tilly public-humiliation thing that I've forgotten all about the beach.

Skirting the front of the castle we get a view over the sea. A tiny group of people are huddling under an umbrella. 'Who's that?' says Jacob. 'What are they doing?'

We cut down across the castle green. It's soggy – boggy actually – and my school shoes are not built for it – so now I'm wet from the top down and the bottom up.

We stop by the pier and look at the beach. No one's lolling around on deckchairs, but Mr Fogg's there in his full yellow sea-going gear. Also, the mayor in a skimpy cagoule, and a couple of reporters. Next to them a white pedalo lies on the sand with two quivering girls shivering next to it.

The mayor's children. They don't go to our school, but I recognise them. They're about our age.

The rain beating on my hood means that I can't hear anything, so I drop down the steps to the sheltered patch of beach under the pier, and take off my hood.

Over the scrunching sound of Jacob's feet on the sand I can just about hear the conversation.

'. . . so I have absolute faith in the beach, proven by my willingness to put my own children, my very own flesh and blood, in one of our 100% safe Bywater-by-Sea pedalos. They'll be out on the sea every day of the summer season . . .'

Mr Fogg nods in agreement, although he looks slightly less happy than the mayor.

'He's not sending them out in this – is he?' says Eric, indicating the rain that has now moved on to torrential. 'They'll drown.'

'That would be interesting,' says Jacob.

We watch the two girls clamber into the pedalo and Albert Fogg push them towards the sea. The journalists are frantically snapping away and I'm wondering if we shouldn't run to the rescue when a wave breaks over the front of the pedalo. The first girl leaps out of the boat and rushes back to the sand, shortly followed by the other.

The mayor argues with them, but they shake their heads in fury and stomp up the beach.

'Phew,' says Eric.

'Pity,' says Jacob.

The next day is sunny, actually warm, and most people run around outside.

'Art Club?' says Mrs Mawes.

'Um,' I say.

It turns out that Art Club is exactly what I feared. An hour of free time wrecked by cutting and sticking. Tilly's there, with Milly and a bunch of friends.

I am the only boy over the age of seven.

'Now, Tom – winner of the Sculpture on the Beach contest – I'm sure you don't need any help from me. Here are some materials, let's see what you can do.'

I stare dumbly at the pots of glue, paint and glitter, and wonder if life can actually get worse.

17

It Takes Twenty-three Coins

When I get home I go up to my bedroom. Some kind of hurricane must have hit it. And then I decide it must be a rabid dog. Or rats. Or a giant squirrel. Chunks of my duvet are missing. My pillow has a hole burrowed right through it. The lampshade is dangling, tattered and torn, and the window, which I closed before I left this morning, has a broken pane of glass.

'What?' I say aloud.

At first I think it must be something that's come in from the outside. An invasion of giant hornets – or birds, or radioactive snakes.

Then I remember the deckchairs.

Frantically I search out the pirate tin. I find it under my bed. It's been torn open from the inside, the metal lid curled back and savaged like a sardine tin. There are no deckchairs inside.

In fact, there are no deckchairs anywhere to be seen. I imagine them marauding and pillaging. Three vicious mousetraps pinching and snapping and tearing. I wonder what kind of damage they'd do.

It would look very much like this.

Eric's dad opens the door. I rush past and race up the stairs to find Eric playing himself at chess.

'What?' he says.

'The deckchairs,' I say, and I explain what's happened.

'Oh, Tom,' he says. He refrains from saying 'You idiot', but I know that's what he means.

'So I've no idea where they are,' I say. 'We need to find them before they get any bigger.'

'How big do you suppose they are now?' he asks.

I hold my hands out, measuring imaginary tiny deckchairs. 'I guess they must be about a credit-card big.'

'Really easy to find then,' he says. 'In a whole town.'

We start in the model village. I know if I was a miniature deckchair that's exactly where I'd hide and I check for the first one I left by the cricket green. It's not there any more. There's no sign of it, not even any damage, and there's no sign of the small ones either. Next, we try the crazy golf. I check all the holes. Eric checks all the Dingly Dell gnomes.

There are no actual deckchairs but something's taken a bite out of one or two of the greens.

'They've been here,' I say.

'But they're not here any more,' says Eric.

We drop down to the sea wall.

Today the sea is glassy and families have come out to enjoy the end of the afternoon sun. The mayor's daughters are pedalling back and forth across the bay. Everything looks calm and lovely.

I lean on the railings and study the beach. 'I suppose they might have tried to get home,' I say.

'Where is home?' says Eric.

'In a sort of cave at the end of the beach,' I say, a sudden thought coming to me. 'Do you suppose there's nothing actually wrong with the beach itself?'

'What do you mean?' asks Eric, catching a wild curl of hair and jamming it under the hook of his glasses.

'Well, I know everything that's happened so far has been on the beach, and we assumed that it must be the sand or the sea or something. But supposing it isn't?'

Eric rubs his chin in a thinking way. 'Where's the cave?' he says in the end.

There are masses of people on the beach. We're weaving our way through the family encampments when a shriek comes from above us on the sea wall.

'AAAAAAAAAARRRRRRRGH!' It's about four million decibels and it comes from a woman and her daughter who race straight down the steps onto the sand and hop about as if they've been stung by something.

'Get off!' screams the girl. 'Beastly thing!'

The mother stares in horror at her daughter and we run over. The child has a smallish deckchair clamped to her piggy nose, much like a large peg. 'Ow! Ow!' squeals the girl.

'Stay still,' says her mother, sticking her fingers into the deckchair and pulling.

'OW! It hurts!' The girl can't stay still and the mother can't get it off.

'Try this,' says Eric, pulling his Field Craft penknife from his pocket. 'We might be able to force it open.' He jams it into the deckchair mechanism and, oyster-like, forces it open.

'Help!' comes a shout from above us on the sea wall.

'Go,' Eric says to me, his fingers dangerously

close to the deckchair's snapping jaws. 'We're good here.'

'Help!'

The cries seem to be coming from the amusement arcade. Amongst all the flashing lights and gurgling games, the owner is standing with his back to the wall, his eyes fixed on the dark space under the machines. I move closer but it's not the space under the machines where the problem lies, it's inside the machine. I press my nose to the glass and see two tiny deckchairs having fun dancing in the tuppence waterfall. They're kicking the coins off the ledges and snip-snapping at the prizes, while the bigger one – the one Eric put under the microscope – is dancing inside the claw machine and throwing itself at the cuddly toys.

I could shrink them, but what good would that do? They'd still be inside the machines, still capable of pinching and biting. I need to get them out.

I rush to the change machine, stuff a pound coin in the top and it spews 2ps into a plastic tub at the bottom. I grab another plastic tub and stick it underneath the machine and then start feeding the coins into the top of the machine. It takes twenty-three coins to get the first cascade, and twelve to get the next, and on the third one of the deckchairs that was teetering on the edge slips over and shoots down into the tub. Before it can even stand up I grab another tub and jam it inside, pinning the chair to the bottom of the first tub.

Eric appears beside me, his hands clasped together, real tears leaking from the corners of his eyes. 'This thing's vicious,' he says, gasping.

'Quick,' I say, picking up another tub, 'drop it in here. It'll work for a few minutes.'

Once we have both the chairs imprisoned we feed more 2ps into the machine. The last tiny deckchair is dancing and leaping and kicking the coins around inside. It seems oblivious to the disappearance of its companion. Just as the man who runs the amusement arcade seems totally ignorant of what has really happened and is still thumping a broom around underneath the machines. He obviously thinks he's looking for an insect.

It takes two more pounds to catch the last deckchair, which tumbles into the tub in a shower of coins, and we jam it under the other two. Then I hold all three together in a quivering sandwich.

'Now that one,' I say, pointing to the claw machine.

The slightly larger chair has fastened itself round a fluffy dragon and is squeezing hard.

'Those things are impossible,' says Eric. 'They never work.'

'Hold this.' I hand him the pile of twitching tubs and grab another pound coin from my pocket.

'Have you only got one left?' asks Eric.

I nod, slot the pound coin in and focus on the claw controls.

'Are you any good at this?' he asks.

'Yes,' I lie.

I've never actually managed to get anything before, but the deckchair has released the dragon and is flipping around inside the machine and the moment I lower the claw it clamps on to one of the open jaws.

'Quick,' says Eric.

Holding my breath I raise the claw and

steer it over the tray.

It dangles there, still inside the machine, swinging and snapping.

'Give it a shove,' I say.

Eric thumps the machine, and the chair sways, swings and gives up its hold. It falls, wriggling and squeaking, until it wedges itself in the slot.

I grab it, pinching it shut while it flexes and squeals.

I feel 88% good, because I'm 12% worried about what to do with it next.

We step out of the arcade. 'Now what?' says Eric. 'We can't drown them – they'll float.'

'No – and I can't shrink them either, there's no point.'

'Jacob,' we say to each other at the same time.

18

Kind of Cute

Going begging to Jacob doesn't come naturally.

'Do you mean you need me?' he says, standing in his front doorway in pants and a vest, rubbing his enormous stomach.

'Yup,' I say. 'We do.'

The deckchairs in the tubs are wibbling and squirming under Eric's fingers. The bigger one is trying hard to escape.

'We need you to destroy these,' says Eric, nodding at the tubs.

'How badly do you need me?' asks Jacob.

Eric and I look at each other. 'Quite badly,'
I say.

'Yes,' says Eric. 'Quite badly.'

'Badly enough to be really nice to me?'

'I don't know,' I say. 'What were you
thinking of?'

'Nice words, perhaps?'

There's a massive kick from the deckchair
I'm holding that I only just manage to hang
on to.

'You're fantastic, marvellous, extraordinary,'
I say.

'Talented, gifted, fairly remarkable,' says Eric.

'Fairly remarkable?' says Jacob. 'Only
fairly?'

'Utterly remarkable,' I say.

'Hmm,' says Jacob. He rubs his stomach
and it moves under his hand in a rolling wave.
'OK,' he says. 'I'll do it.'

* * *

I've never been in Jacob's house before. It's not how I expected. Because his mum is big and pink and marshmallowy, I thought that the house would be the same. A grown-up version of the kind of thing Tilly would like.

But it's not like that at all. It's modern and white and clean-lined and really quite nice. Or it would be if the sitting room wasn't basically just a huge TV set.

We go up to Jacob's bedroom, which is exactly what I expected, crammed full of technology and old crisp packets. Jacob empties a load of sweet wrappers from a tin onto the floor.

'You can't do that,' says Eric.

'S'all right, Mum'll tidy it up later.'

'But . . .' Eric begins.

I hold my hand up. Eric sighs and takes the top tub out of the column of tubs.

The little deckchair snaps upright and tries to get out, Eric tips the tub and the deckchair falls into the steep-sided metal tin.

'Coo,' says Jacob. 'It's like a little animal.'

'Very like,' says Eric, taking the next tub from the stack and dropping the next deckchair in.

We watch the two deckchairs lying down, standing up, snapping and trying to get out.

'They're like little tigers,' I say.

'Or crocodiles,' says Eric, dropping the third one in.

I drop my bigger one in and it chases the other three round. Much like a sheepdog.

'So what next?' says Jacob.

'We burn them,' I say.

We all look down at the little deckchairs thumping and throwing themselves about.

'Really?' says Jacob. 'Burn them – like they are just ordinary deckchairs or something?'

'Yes,' I say, holding the tin firmly to my stomach.

We stare for the longest while.

'They're kind of cute,' says Jacob.

'In a vicious snappy way,' says Eric, rubbing a red patch on his palm. 'But yes, they are.'

I look up at the other two. 'We can't, can we? We can't burn them.' They both stare at me. 'Let's give it another day. Think about it for a while.'

'Yes.' Eric nods.

'Right,' I say. 'I just need somewhere safe to leave them overnight.'

19

Not Kind of Cute

I can hear the tiny deckchairs dancing around inside the tin and I'd really like to take them straight to the little town lock-up, which we agreed would be the safest place for them. It's not a prison any more, it's a tourist attraction, but it does have iron bars and a letter box and nothing inside. And Grandma has a key.

But we need to wait until dark, and we need to take a look inside the cave at the end of the beach.

The last of the holidaymakers are leaving, and Eric, Jacob and I try to look as if we're beachcombing.

I don't really get beachcombing – it's all rubbish, some of it's bone rubbish and some of it's plastic rubbish – but I try to be convincing.

The mayor's daughters climb out of the pedalo, rubbing their legs. He greets them on the shore and the larger one shouts something at him and waves her arms violently, which I imagine means something like *I'm not doing that any more.*

With a miserable face, the mayor drags the pedalo back up the beach and leaves it chained to the wall. He doesn't put it in the cave.

The remains of some of the sculptures are still visible on the beach. A sand dragon that has lost its head and half a mermaid, between all the flattened patches and new sandcastles. Jacob kicks the head from the mermaid, tramples the dragon flat and knocks down the largest castle. He's very similar to a windbreak at times.

Albert Fogg drags the last deckchairs towards the cave and I pretend to examine a really interesting pile of bladderwrack. Eric joins me. 'See,' I say. 'Over there.' I point towards the door in the side of the sea wall.

We crouch on the beach, watching and waiting. Albert Fogg rummages in his overalls for a key.

'What's he doing?' asks Jacob, arriving panting behind us.

'Quick,' I say, 'let's get a look inside.'

We stroll and then gallop until we're close enough to see, but far enough away for Mr Fogg not to notice us.

The door swings open and he shines a torch through the opening. I can't see exactly what's going on, but things are moving inside.

'Did you see that?' I say to Eric.

He nods.

Albert Fogg arms himself with a broom and goes in bellowing. 'Get back, you nasty things, you. Get BACK!' There's a crack and bang and Mr Fogg rushes out clutching his elbow. He tries to shut the door but a windbreak jams itself in the hinge and he can't.

'You beastly things, get back – or I'll destroy the lot of you.' The beach equipment inside his store doesn't seem to be able to hear and starts to stagger onto the beach.

'Help!' he yells, slipping backwards as a huge deckchair with an extra leg-rest topples towards him.

I get there just as the cloth of the deckchair starts to smother his face. 'Pull,' I shout to Eric, and we both grab the leg-rest end and tug violently until Mr Fogg struggles free from underneath.

The deckchair joins its brothers stamping out of the cave and standing on their ends on the beach.

Jacob dances back and forth in front of them looking big, his eyes flashing dangerously red.

More and more of the chairs march out of the store, until they're five deep on the beach, and then the first one finds the steps at the back and tries to climb them.

We watch in horror as it manages to get halfway up towards the promenade.

'Oh no,' says Mr Fogg, sinking his face into his hands and moaning. 'I'm done for,' he says, collapsing onto the beach and pulling his coat up over his head.

I check the beach – it's empty – and Mr Fogg can't see, so I wave at Jacob and he lets loose a long tongue of flame, which bounces across the deckchairs, crackling, singeing and sparking, but not really burning.

The chair on the steps pauses.

'Again,' shouts Eric, already beginning to drip from his fingertips.

The heat is immense as Jacob sends lightning bolt after lightning bolt at the chairs, and then Eric counters this by sprinkling them with water. A wall of steam rises from the beach and the chairs stop, evidently confused and hopefully intimidated.

'I can shrink them,' I say. 'But it won't really help.'

'We can burn them this time,' says Jacob.

'They're not a bit cute.'

'They're still living beings, and they're Mr Fogg's deckchairs,' says Eric. 'They're his livelihood.'

The deckchairs stand facing us. Shuffling. Waiting.

Mr Fogg is still sitting on the beach, his face hidden. Waiting as well.

And then, as if someone switched them off, the deckchairs sag to the sand, tumbling, flopping, leaning and ultimately lying just as deckchairs should, awkward and floppy.

20

Foggis Fogg was the First

We go with Mr Fogg to the Trusty Tramper, the café in the harbour that the sailors use.

'The usual, Albert?' asks Cheery Charlie, the woman that runs the place.

'Aye,' says Mr Fogg, wiping his nose on his yellow sou'wester coat and shaking his head.

She provides him with a mug of tea and we cluster around a small yellow table by the door.

'So when did it start, Mr F?' asks Eric, arranging sugar.

Mr Fogg stares long and hard at the tiny wisp of steam rising from his cup.

'January. No – March.' He takes off his cap and scratches his head. 'Or was it before Christmas?' He stares out of the window at the approaching darkness. 'February it was. February, just as I got them out for a bit of a clean-up. That's when I noticed something was up.'

'What kind of thing?' I ask.

'Well.' Mr Fogg sips his tea and sits back. 'It's difficult to say. There was a bit of this and a bit of that.'

Jacob lets a long whistle out from between his front teeth. 'Let me know if you find anything out,' he says, standing up. 'I'm just going to get a hot chocolate.'

I check my pockets for change. I've no money.

I try again. 'What kind of thing – exactly?'

'At the start of the season I like to check the chairs, wash 'em down, clean up the pedalos, see there's no mouse holes in the windbreaks – that sort of thing.'

'Oh yes,' I say.

'So it was a sunny day, and I opened up the shed there, and pulled out one or two chairs and they were – frisky.'

'Frisky?'

'Yes – frisky. Dancing about a bit in the wind, harder to pick up, put down and fold. I didn't think anything of it, but then the next time I opened it up, probably about a week later, one of the chairs sort of fell – well, launched itself at me.'

'Oh?'

'And then, during Easter, it's been getting worse. I found the ones at the side of the store were less of a problem, but the ones towards the back have been the worst – so uppity – and as the season's gone on I've had to hire out more of them, and now I've had to use the difficult ones or disappoint people.'

'So what's causing it?' asks Eric.

'Search me,' he says, blowing on his cup. 'No idea – kept the chairs in that lock-up all my life. Nothing's been in, nothing's changed.'

'And have you found any way to stop them?' I ask, thinking of the four little chairs still jammed in Jacob's sweet tin, which are dancing around under my blazer, letting out occasional crashings and bangings.

Mr Fogg shakes his head. 'No,' he says. 'All I've managed to do is to truss them up or tie them down. I've never seen them go quiet like those ones you saw on the beach just now – it's as if they're alive.'

'Shouldn't be using them,' says Eric. 'I mean, someone's going to get hurt sooner or later.'

'I agree,' says Mr Fogg. 'I tried to say that to the mayor – I said, "Someone's going to get hurt sooner or later" – and he said we had to keep it quiet.'

'I get that it would be bad for trade,' I say.

'It's not just that,' says Mr Fogg. 'It's the Best Beach contest.'

'I can see it would be nice to win it . . .'

'No – you don't understand. He's *desperate* to win it. He's attracted all these big businesses. Did you know that there's a big burger chain from America sniffing around Marigold Tours? Or that the Royal Hotel could soon be known as the Royal Gogleplex Hotel? It's already been sold. Also, he's selling off the beach and the rights to sell deckchairs. He's got a Chinese sofa company in mind – apparently people want something more comfortable these days – AND, in order for those deals to go through, we need to win the Best Beach contest.'

'Oh!' says Eric.

'I don't understand,' I say. 'Why are you keeping it a secret? If he's selling it off, what would you be doing? Won't it be the end of your job?'

'Ah – thing is, they'd let me stop at last. Been trying to retire for the last few years. I've got me a little web-design company in Regis Bottom that I'd love to have more time with. But they keep on asking me back. Been Foggs doing the deckchairs since 1875, you know. Foggis Fogg was the very first, then it was his son, Foggit Fogg . . .'

'But wouldn't you be sad at seeing the deckchairs go after so many generations?' asks Eric.

Mr Fogg stares into space. 'Honestly – not much. I'm pretty fed up with it.'

Eric looks a little weepy-eyed.

'Well,' says Mr Fogg, relenting, 'I'd miss it, of course I would, for about five minutes, but, imagine, I've almost never felt grass beneath my feet on a sunny day, always blasted sand between my toes. Plays merry hell with my corns.'

'You must have had some pretty terrific summers on the beach?' I say.

'Seventy-six was good – and then we had a lovely time in eighty-two.' He sips his tea. 'Yes. I don't want to do it, but I suppose it's a tradition for the town.'

Jacob sits back down with a mug of steaming-hot chocolate. It smells divine. I think of Grandma's promised tripe à la mode de Caen, and feel even hungrier.

'And what about you?' I ask Mr Fogg. 'Do you want to win the Best Beach competition? Does it mean anything to you?'

Mr Fogg examines the back of his hand. 'It would be the pinnacle of my career,' he says carefully. 'Yes – I would like to win it.'

'So, if I've got this right – if the deckchairs behave themselves, we'll win the Best Beach contest and end up with them replaced by sofas from some multinational company from Shanghai, and if they don't . . .?' I trail off.

Mr Fogg raises his eyebrow. 'Who knows?

'So,' says Eric. 'Can we have a look in the storage cave?'

21

Is That a Bad Thing?

Mr Fogg has a fantastic set of torches.
Most of them must be left over from the
Victorians. 'Ready?' he says, and he unlocks
the padlock.

We stand in the doorway waiting to be
attacked, our eyes acclimatising to the gloom.

'What are we looking for?' asks Jacob,
stepping through the door.

'Signs of life – anything odd really,'
says Eric.

'Do you mind if I stay here?' says Mr Fogg,

loitering in the entrance with a broom. 'Just in case any of the beggars make a run for it.' He looks scared.

I put my tin down by the entrance. The four deckchairs inside have gone quite quiet. Perhaps they're asleep. I'm conscious that I need to get rid of them soon, before they grow any more. I can't handle four full-sized mad creatures in my bedroom.

I shine my torch into the store. Cobwebs festoon the vaulted ceiling.

'Not really a cave, so much as a cellar,' mutters Eric.

Jacob pushes through the front line of chairs, the ones we hastily stacked inside after he and Eric subdued them. They smell of wet bonfires, and are totally passive. Behind them, something scuttles.

I stop, listening and watching the nearest

cobweb flex under the weight of a particularly heavy spider.

The scuttling stops.

I push my way past the scorched chairs and stop by a collection of dusty windbreaks. They aren't moving, but it feels as if they're watching me.

'Tom?' says Eric from my right. 'Are you there?'

I stumble between two lobster pots, reaching Eric's side, and look into the pool of torchlight.

A beach volleyball set is limboing around itself, over and under, knotting and unknotting. He shines the light higher and reveals a huge dripping crack in the wall. A gash with bright green mossy sides.

'What is it?' asks Jacob, appearing beside us. 'Is it an alien?'

'No – I don't think so,' says Eric. 'But it is a cleft in the rock.'

'Through which water is running,' I say.

Jacob looks at us, shining his torch from his chin upwards making a ghost pig face. 'I don't understand.'

On the way home, Jacob walks backwards.

It's annoying, but then practically everything about Jacob is annoying. The only person more annoying than Jacob is Tilly. I remember home and humiliation and forget feeling hungry.

'So why's the rock important?' he asks again.

'It's a meteorite,' says Eric patiently. 'The same meteorite that makes everything around here behave so oddly.'

'Oh,' says Jacob, thumping backwards over a kerb.

His brain cogs come up with the next question. 'So what's the water got to do with it?'

Eric sighs. 'I think, and it's only a theory, that the meteorite dust, all the stuff that was mined last year, is dissolving in the groundwater and then dripping into Mr Fogg's store.'

'So we could stop it happening then – couldn't we?' asks Jacob.

'Possibly, but I'm not sure we want to,' I say.

'Why?' says Jacob.

'Because if the beach wins the Best Beach award, they'll sell it off to someone – it'll be covered in plastic sofas and takeaways and then it won't be the same any more.'

'Is that a bad thing?' asks Jacob.

'Yes,' we say in chorus.

22

If It's All Under Control?

Jacob goes home to a tea of sausage, mash and beans.

Eric and I walk on in almost total darkness and empty the tin of deckchairs through the letter box into the tiny lock-up. I just hope that Mrs Santos who keeps it doesn't go in for a few days. I wouldn't want her to be attacked.

'Why did they give up?' says Eric.

'What – who?'

'The chairs. I don't understand why they gave up on the beach like that. It was like a full-scale battle and then suddenly they lay down and surrendered.'

'Perhaps it was the combination of fire and water – like steam-cleaning.'

'You're probably right,' says Eric. 'So what shall we do about it? We can't leave it like it is. Poor Mr Fogg, he wants to win the contest, but he's having a terrible time and the beach is downright dangerous.'

'We could move all the chairs, steam-clean them, seal up the hole and solve it . . .'

'But that would mean that the mayor could sell it all off and Bywater-by-Sea just wouldn't be Bywater-by-Sea any more.'

We stand in the darkness listening to the sand fleas hopping all over the beach in the dark.

'It's the mayor – we need a new one – properly elected. I think it's time we got your dad and my mum to join forces.'

'Really?' says Eric. 'You'd do that?'

I think of the combined embarrassment factor and then I think about Bywater-by-Sea and the whole town sold to a plastic corporation and say, 'Really.'

'So we thought that perhaps you might like to work together,' I say to Mum who is combing nits from Tilly's hair into a salad bowl full of shampoo and frantically paddling head lice.

'OW!' screams Tilly. 'What? Mum team up with Colin Threepwood? Per-leaze. That is not happening.'

'Tilly!' barks Mum. 'That's none of your business.' She yanks the comb through Tilly's hair. 'Although – I'm not sure I think it's a good idea.'

'Because you've given up all hope of becoming mayor?' says Tilly hopefully.

Mum pulls extra hard on Tilly's hair. 'No – that's not it.' But she doesn't say why.

I suspect that, in spite of Mum and Dad's bravado, Tilly's little trick with the baby photos and the karaoke has sort of worked. Mum is feeling dented.

'You see,' says Eric, 'we think that together you could pool your voters and get enough people on board to defeat the current mayor.'

Tilly swings round. 'You are not serious! Surely. I can't think of anything, anything at all, that would be worse for my image at school.'

We all stare at Tilly. She goes bright red.

'Because the current mayor is not good for the town. We overheard –' I look at Eric, who nods – 'we sort of overheard that he's selling off the beach, the Royal Hotel and probably some other places.'

Mum puts down the nit comb. 'Who to?'

'Global conglomerates,' says Eric.

'Sofa companies,' I say.

She looks at Eric, her mouth hanging open. 'Does your dad know this?'

'No,' says Eric. 'I don't think so.'

Mum rushes to the sink to wash the nit gloop from her fingers. 'I think we'd better tell him.'

'What about me?' says Tilly plaintively from underneath her louse-infested conditioner. 'I'm only half done – I've still got nits.'

'What about you?' says Mum, grabbing my and Eric's arms. 'Come on, boys, let's go.'

'Don't mention anything about the crazed deckchairs,' I mutter to Eric as we scuttle up the hill to his house. 'Because, you know, it's just easier if she doesn't know.'

'Mum's the word,' he says, zipping his lips.

Eric and I pretend to eat alfalfa and peanut falafels in the kitchen while Mum talks earnestly to Eric's dad over the table and drinks quinoa juice.

Eric's dad nods wisely as Mum outlines her attack. 'Mayor and vice mayor, Colin,' she says. 'You can be the front man – everyone loves you. I'll be the administrator – how does that sound?'

'You mean we run together? We enter this bold new part of our lives in tandem?'

Mum raises her eyebrows. 'Sort of,' she says.

'It seems to be working,' says Eric. 'They're getting on. But what are we going to do about the chairs? The election isn't until next week. Someone'll be killed between now and then.'

'But the Best Beach contest is this weekend, on Saturday.' I try to swallow a particularly solid piece of falafel. 'We have to keep the chairs in order so they don't kill anyone, but let them be just uncomfortable enough to make the beach a less lovely spot. I suppose after that we can try to cure them.'

'Let's hope it rains so that no one goes onto the beach until we do.'

Mum and I go home and she spends the evening printing Eric's dad's name alongside hers on all the dayglo posters. When she tells Dad and Grandma about the mayor's plans they're horrified.

'But that's awful!' says Dad.

'It explains a lot of things,' says Grandma. 'All those people with clipboards, and the sudden price hike in the Curl Up and Dye hairdressers – and other things.' She stares at me.

Dad makes soup and Grandma and Mum line up loads of posters. The only person who doesn't help is Tilly, who sticks her tongue out, says she'd never eat Dad's soup even if he paid her, looks murderously at Mum, and goes off scratching her head to torture her Woodland Friends.

Grandma offers to stick the new posters all over town in the dark.

'Tom, dear, you can help,' she says, grabbing a handful of posters and a load of tape.

'Can I?' I say.

'Oh yes, we'll do a better job together.'

'So,' says Grandma when we're outside. 'Can you shrink those two there?'

'Shrink?' Grandma hates me shrinking things.

'Yup,' she says. 'We can paste them up on the model village houses. We're open this weekend and people will see them.'

'If you're sure,' I say, making an O with my thumb and forefinger round the posters.

Click.

The two posters shrink to about the size of a matchbox and I hand one to Grandma and we tape them to the front of the tiny church.

There's a huge desert of silence while we leave the model village and walk out into the empty high street. I hold the posters while she tapes one to a telegraph pole.

'So how's poor Mr Fogg?' she says in the end.

'Fine, fine – I imagine.'

'Just that I gathered from Cheerful Charlie in the café that you'd been in with him and he seemed quite shaken.'

'Oh,' I say. 'Yes.' Grandma knows everything in this town. Everything. So there's no point in lying. 'He's struggling.'

'With the beach furniture?'

'Yes,' I say. Trying to keep it minimal.

'Right,' says Grandma. 'And what are you doing about it?'

'It's all under control,' I say.

'Good,' she says, sticking the last poster on the village horse trough. 'So long as you've got it under control we'll be fine. But if you need help, Tom, dear, do let me know.'

23

No Problem

For two days, while Mum and Colin Threepwood bombard the town with contradictory but well-meaning slogans, like SMALL IS WHERE THE HEART IS and LONG LIVE THE BIG PRIVATELY OWNED HOTEL, it rains.

But on Wednesday the sun comes out.

I leave really early.

'Don't you want breakfast, Tom?' asks Dad, waving a saucepan.

'Er – no. I'll grab some on the way,' I say, leaving Dad in his pyjamas, making toast.

I race down the street, passing the milkman and the postman, aware that I have almost never seen the town this early in the morning.

I get to the beach at about the same time as Mr Fogg who is standing outside his store jangling his keys and looking anxious. 'Ah, Tom,' he says. 'Just plucking up the courage.'

'Could we leave the deckchairs off the beach?' I say.

He shakes his head. 'The beach inspectors are already in town. The chairs have to be out.'

'But if the beach is wrong, then they'll think we're no good. We won't win the contest and it won't be sold off.'

Mr Fogg looks out through the tiny gap in his face behind which his eyes lurk. 'No – not on my watch. So long as it's still my job, I'll do it properly,' he says. 'And besides – I want to win it.'

'Really?' I ask.

He scratches his bottom in reply.

'Well, in that case, we'll try to run a rota, so that one of us is here with you at all times. We'll try to help you win it.'

'Would you do that?' he says, sounding almost hopeful.

'Yes – er – no problem,' I say.

It's not 'no problem'. It's practically impossible. Even with my bike, coming and going from school is tricky.

'So, class,' says Mr Bell, 'we're going to look at another aspect of empathetic behaviour. Today we're going to try to imagine what someone else is thinking. And I've brought someone small to help.'

He opens the door, and picks up a basket from outside. The basket quivers and then immediately starts wailing.

A baby?

'Yes, I've brought Gemma with me. Cootchy, cootchy, little bubble baby.'

Mr Bell blows bubbles at the baby and the baby smiles and blows bubbles back. 'Snoodly, snoodly, snoodly.' Mr Bell rubs noses with the baby.

At the back of the class, Jacob makes retching noises.

'So,' says Mr Bell, clearing his throat. 'So, I'd like you to look into Gemma's eyes and tell me what you think she's thinking. How you think she's feeling. Oh – where's Eric Threepwood? He'd be good at this.'

'Just gone to the toilet, Mr Bell, sir,' I lie. 'I'll go and find him if you like.'

'Or I will,' says Jacob, glancing at the baby and her adoring fans and backing towards the door.

'No, no, I'll go,' I say, lunging through it. I practically throw myself into the pasta maps of the London Underground and race out of the school and onto my bike.

I freewheel round the front of the castle and down to the beach. 'Hi!' I shout to Eric. He's sitting outside Mr Fogg's cave under a huge beach umbrella. 'All quiet?'

Eric grabs his school bag and takes the bike off me. 'Small moment with an inflatable dolphin and a granny but we won and it's safely back in the cave.'

The rest of Wednesday passes quietly.

Thursday starts with drizzle.

All three of us go to school.

First we do art.

Miss Mawes looks at my 'Woman in Blue', turns it round, examines it upside down and says, 'Very interesting to see you using Picasso's mask techniques. Have you been reading up on them?'

I look at my biro scrawl. I couldn't have made it worse if I'd tried.

'Brilliant,' says Miss Mawes, sailing off to examine Jacob's masterpiece, 'Woman in Red'.

Today there's no baby, and we're doing physics, but the cardigan's back. Mr Bell has a kettle, a bowl of ice and a glass. He's discussing thermal shock. It's all fine, and then somehow he brings it round to empathy.

He pulls on yellow rubber gloves and safety goggles. 'Stand back, everyone,' he bellows, and then, as if he remembers himself: 'Please.'

With great concentration he boils the kettle. 'So if we were being kind to our glass, we'd warm it up slowly – but if we want to shatter it – we plunge it from hot to cold.' Which is exactly what he does, and the glass pings apart in a not terribly interesting way, mixing shards of glass with blocks of ice.

'Anyway,' says Mr Bell, staring into the bowl hopefully as if something spectacular could happen at this late stage. 'Anyway.' He sighs, peeling off the rubber gloves and sitting sideways on the desk. One leg just touching the floor. 'I've managed to get my hands on this wonderful computer game.'

Jacob, who has been staring into the bowl of ice waiting for something to happen, wakes and looks around. 'Did he say computer game?'

'Yes, young Jacob. Computer game. It's called *Cuddle or Destroy*, and it's designed to help you make the right choices in life. So who's first on the computers then?'

Jacob gets in first, of course. 'What do I do here then?' he says, as a small green lizard-alien thing races towards him.

'Presumably you have to decide whether to cuddle or –' starts Eric, but before he's even finished the sentence, Jacob has annihilated the alien, leaving a green smear on the virtual landscape and losing a life.

'I get it,' says Jacob. 'I should have killed him the moment I saw him.'

I glance out of the window. The drizzle has dried up and there's an ominous patch of blue sky over the playground. 'I'd better go,' I say to Eric.

He nods and patiently explains to Jacob the meaning of the word 'cuddle'.

The beach is quiet. Full of holidaymakers, and one or two people with clipboards, but no sign of marauding beach furniture.

24

Jacob vs Deckchairs

Friday dawns sunny and threatens to be hot.

'Expecting a high of seventy-six degrees in the Bywater Regis area, clear skies and light winds . . .' says the weatherman on the radio.

Grandma looks at me over her specs. 'Still OK there, Tom? Managing to stay in school every day?'

'Yes,' I reply, my voice strangled by the lie.

I race to school on my bike. Jacob's taken the first shift.

'He's not well, the poor little mite,' says

Mr Bell. 'Let's spare a moment to send him good thoughts.'

I imagine Jacob sitting on the beach eating ice cream and think dark thoughts. I only hope he's taking the job seriously.

We limp through to lunchtime, gazing into each other's eyes and imagining each other's feelings.

'Tom looks really weird, sir,' says Petra Boyle. Which is a bit much coming from someone wearing dental braces obviously designed by a concrete engineer.

At lunch, Eric and I hang out at the bins waiting for Jacob. But he doesn't come.

'Do you think he's run into trouble?' asks Eric.

'I think we should check,' I say.

Getting past Dad in the playground is easy. He's asked for the reasons behind a fight and two girls are shouting and pointing at each other and Dad's looking confused and trying to get them to talk quietly and slowly.

It's not worth asking. I could have told him that.

We aren't even at the beach when the noise hits us.

Yowls and yells and screams.

'It's happening!' shouts Eric as we pick up speed past the harbour and onto the sea wall.

I stall for a moment at the top of the steps and look down.

The deckchairs have mutinied. It's mayhem. All the families are running around in circles trying to reclaim their possessions from the snapping jaws of the chairs. Right through the middle races a small child pursued by a single beach umbrella, both of them skipping over the sandcastles, clearing everyone to the sides.

Everyone, that is, except Jacob. He's standing in the centre, red-faced and sweaty, sending bolts of flame at the rebellious chairs. Sparks are rising, but the chairs don't seem to be bothered. They tramp and stamp and kick sand into the air, and then finally, when he sends out a fireball, they notice him, turning their attention to him rather than the holidaymakers. There's a moment's pause while the chairs form ranks and lines and all swing to face the same way.

Jacob suddenly looks very small.

'Oh dear,' say Eric. 'We'd better help.'

I'm about to run with him to join Jacob, when I hear a muffled cry. I look round to see who's in trouble. It's Mr Fogg trapped inside his giant parasol, cursing and shouting.

'Mr Fogg,' I cry, peeling back the layers of the parasol. 'Are you all right?'

The parasol fights me, tightening itself round him until all I can see are his wellington boots sticking out of the bottom.

The whole thing is still upright but wriggling, and I can't tell if it's him moving or the parasol itself. I turn to see if Eric might be able to help but all I can make out is steam rising from the middle of the beach, until a figure emerges from the smoke.

It's not Eric or Jacob, it's the mayor, and he's shouting at the escaping tourists. 'But it's a great place. Don't go! Stay. We're so much better than Bywater Regis.'

'Stop!' he shouts, waving his arms at a small child, who shrieks and runs faster.

'Come back.' The mayor struggles up the steps onto the sea wall and pleads with a family who rush straight for the bus stop, pushing him away.

'Stay,' he says to a woman dragging her weeping child along the pavement.

I turn back to the parasol. Mr Fogg is making choking sounds, and the parasol has closed so tightly on him that I can see his face quite clearly through the cloth. His mouth is open, pressed against the fabric.

'Wait a sec,' I shout, fumbling through my pockets until I find a biro. 'Open your mouth as wide as possible,' I say and I wriggle the pen into the cloth. The point pierces between the threads, pushing them to the sides and making an airway for Mr Fogg. As I do so, the cloth of the parasol bunches, and as if he was an irritation the parasol shoots Albert Fogg from its tasselled bottom onto the sand.

'Oh my!' he coughs. 'That was close.' Next

to him the parasol billows, flaps and furls itself tight. It appears to be sulking.

I glance over to the dissipating cloud of steam.

A heap of beach furniture lies motionless. Eric and Jacob are circling it and watching it carefully, the occasional jet of either fire or water dousing the steaming mass of wood and stripy cloth and plastic.

'Oh lumme,' says Mr Fogg, scratching his bottom. 'That's done it. We'll never win anything now.'

25

Scrambled Egg (1)

We have to work really hard to get the beach cleaned up. All night, in fact.

And I have to tell Grandma.

Who tells Eric's dad, who, it turns out, is really good at scrubbing deckchairs.

'Remind me why we're doing this,' says Jacob, managing a steady warm hand-dryer heat over the parasols that Eric and his dad have scrubbed ready for steaming.

'Because we want to win the Best Beach contest,' says Eric.

'But I thought we didn't want to win.' Jacob's eyes flash red as he adds heat to Eric's fine spray of water and steams another pile of parasols.

'Mr Fogg wants to win,' says Eric patiently, 'but we don't want the big businesses to take over the town. We need to make the beach inspectors think that everything's perfect, but make life uncomfortable for the international conglomerates.'

Which gives me a brilliant idea.

'Have we washed everything?' I say.

'Well, apart from that lot over there.' Eric points at a last pile of chairs, flexing under a large tarpaulin.

'Fine, job well done,' says Grandma, opening up a thermos and pouring everyone a slightly blobby paper cup of hot chocolate. 'Almost there, chaps.'

'I'll clean up the last few,' I say, 'if Eric will stay. You take Mr Fogg home, Grandma – we'll finish up.'

Grandma gives me a hard stare. 'If you're sure, Tom.'

'I'm sure,' I say.

'I'm sure too,' says Jacob. 'Beddy-byes for meeeeee. Night, all.' And he wanders off the beach up towards the town, sending little sparks from his feet as he walks.

Grandma takes Mr Fogg by the elbow. 'Come on, Albert, get yourself a few hours' sleep before the crowds arrive.'

'What crowds?' says Mr Fogg. 'No one'll come after all this chaos – will they?'

'They'll come,' says Grandma reassuringly. 'Don't you worry.'

'If you think so.' Mr Fogg shakes his head. 'And I can't believe all that steam – how did we get all that steam?' He looks puzzled.

'Well, Albert . . .' I hear Grandma making up stories to explain Jacob's and Eric's powers as she and Mr Fogg stagger over the sands towards the steps. 'It's like this . . .'

'What are we doing with these, Tom?' asks Eric, pointing at the chairs left in the heap.

'This,' I say, forming an O with my finger and thumb, and taking a sighting on them.

Click.

The tiny chairs and tarpaulin lie in the palm of my hand, snapping and wriggling.

Eric peers over my shoulder, looks up at me and raises an eyebrow. 'What exactly do you have in mind?'

The first strip of dawn light hovers in the east as we scuttle along the promenade towards the Royal Hotel.

'It was what you said about making life uncomfortable for the international conglomerates.'

'Yes?'

We stop at the back of the hotel. 'You were absolutely right. That's what we need to do, so that's what we are doing. Open the door.'

Eric tugs at the door handle as if he's expecting it to bite him and we stand in the opening looking in at the kitchen. The lights are on, and pots and pans are simmering, but it appears to be empty.

'Go on,' I say, gripping the deckchairs tightly in my hands.

'But aren't we trespassing?'

'This is an emergency. We're allowed to trespass,' I say, tiptoeing past him into the kitchen. We pause, listening by spitting pans full of bacon. 'I can't hear anyone – let's go on to the hall.'

'Really?' Eric's gone snot-pale.

The huge hallway is empty except for a vacuum cleaner and a radio playing quietly in the corner. There's another sound, a kind of whispering, rubbing sound and I realise it's Eric shaking, his springs of hair trembling against each other.

'Bung one over there somewhere,' I say, nodding towards the receptionist's desk.

In the same way that you would pick up a crab, Eric takes a single deckchair from my hand and places it in the desk drawer.

He lets out a silly little giggle and clamps his fingers over his mouth. 'Sorry,' he says. 'Where next?'

We slip into the housekeeping room and drop three more in the trolleys that chambermaids use to clean up rooms.

'And one in here,' says Eric, dropping one in the umbrella stand.

Finally, as we sneak out of the kitchen, we slip one more in the scrambled eggs and another in the cereal.

Eric beams as we step out into the street. 'That's the naughtiest thing I've ever done,' he says, grinning and clapping his hands. 'I loved it.'

I open my hand. 'We've still got these,' I say, looking at six more deckchairs and a parasol. 'If you want to do some more?'

'Marigold's,' he says. 'Didn't Mr Fogg say there was a burger chain interested?'

The streets are still empty and the seagulls are setting out for a day's squawking as we head down the quay towards the boat-booking kiosk.

A fisherman nods to us as we saunter along the harbour wall. He doesn't look at us for long – he's too busy mending his nets – so we're able to get really close to the Marigold Tours boats.

It takes no more than a minute to drop three deckchairs on each boat and the parasol into a cabin and then step away.

'Right,' says Eric. 'Is that it then?'

'Yes – let's go home, get some sleep and meet again in a few hours.'

I don't get anything like as much sleep as I need.

'You are failing in your duty as a brother!' Tilly bellows, slamming my bedroom door open and kicking my carefully constructed model of the International Space Station out of the window.

'Hey!' I shout, trying to wake up and protect myself against more damage.

'Well, you are – you're pathetic.' Six months' collection of bottle tops follows the ISS into the garden. 'You haven't made them stop!'

She stares at me, her hair wild, her hands on hips.

I can't summon the words, so Tilly goes on.

'They're compounding it. They're making it worse – she's running with HIM!' She points in the general direction of Eric's house. 'And Dad –' Tilly pinches her face into a dismal on-the-edge-of-tears frown – 'I can't bear another day at school with him there.' She sits on my bed and does a long drawn-out sob.

I think she's forgotten that it's me – that I don't fall for this stuff.

'Um,' I say in the end.

'Tom,' she says pitifully. 'Save me.' She melts towards me, laying her head very close to mine. Snuggling up, her hair lying across my pillow. Our cheeks touch.

I open my mouth to say something profound and comforting, nearly say something mean and from the heart, and decide that probably the best policy is to say nothing at all.

Only then do I remember she still has head lice.

26

Good Old Jacob

Bleary-eyed and immediately itchy, I stumble through breakfast with Mum and Dad and then stagger on down to the beach.

I expect to meet Grandma on the way but there's no sign of her.

The deckchairs are looking perfect. Well, almost perfect. There's a faint aroma of charcoal and one or two darkened struts, but they're pretty good all the same.

Mr Fogg is sitting under his parasol sipping tea, and a lone family has set up camp and is building the first sandcastle of the day.

It is the picture of happy beachness. Except that there's hardly anyone there.

'Mornin', Tom,' says Mr Fogg.

'Morning, Mr Fogg – are the inspectors here yet?'

Mr Fogg looks at his watch. 'Due any minute now.' And right on cue three people dressed in a most unbeachy way arrive at the top of the steps. A pointy woman with pointy glasses and pointy shoes, flanked by two men in grey suits: one carrying a camera, the other a picnic hamper.

I sit with Mr Fogg under the umbrella and watch.

Another family drifts onto the beach. I recognise them; they're local.

'It'll be in the papers today,' Mr Fogg mutters. 'No one'll come. You'll see.'

For an agonising half hour, sun beats down on the sand and the inspectors sit in deckchairs surrounded by acres of space.

'Perhaps it's really good that it's empty,' I say.

Mr Fogg shakes his head. 'Don't think so.'

We watch the inspectors take samples of sand and water, examine the beach toilets, and then home in on the two families.

They're just approaching the second family when Eric arrives and joins us under the brolly. 'Not many people,' he says.

'No,' I say, watching the embarrassing exchange between the inspectors and the people on the beach.

'Never gonna win it – end of my career here and we'll never win the prize.' Mr Fogg lets out a long sad sigh.

And then something wonderful happens.

As if someone's turned on a tap, family after family stream down the steps. Soon most of the available sand is replaced by towels and buckets and spades, and within minutes, the sea teems with splashing toddlers and children on inflatables.

'Can we hire a pedalo?' Petra Boyle rushes up to me holding out a five-pound note.

'Er – yes,' I say, pulling one from against the wall and heaving it down to the sea.

Eric hires out another one, and soon we've run out.

As the last beach volleyball set goes, Jacob arrives, ice cream in hand. 'Wotcha – how's it going?'

'See for yourself,' I say, scratching my head. 'Have a good night's sleep?'

'Yes and no – your gran had me busy from six this morning.' Jacob pulls a smug face.

He knows something I don't and he knows it's annoying.

'What did she have you busy doing, may I ask?' says Eric, asking the question I want to ask, but don't want Jacob to know that I want to ask – if you see what I mean.

'Leafleting,' he says. 'An ordinary job for someone with such superior powers as myself, but, as she said – vital to the well-being of the town.' The smugness is almost suffocating.

'Oh?' says Eric. 'What were the leaflets for?'

'Here's one,' says Jacob, pulling a scrumpled piece of paper from his pocket.

FREE ENTRY TO THE MODEL VILLAGE AND A FREE ROUND OF CRAZY GOLF FOR EVERYONE WHO GETS THIS STAMPED ON THE BEACH ON SATURDAY – AMALTHEA PERKS.

'Flip!' I say.

'Wow,' says Eric. 'Wow and wow to the wow squared.'

'Good old Grandma,' I say, and feel about 100% good. And then I remember Dad and Mum and Tilly and feel about 78% good.

'And good old me,' says Jacob.

'Of course,' says Eric. 'Good old Jacob.'

27

Scrambled Egg (2)

We stamp leaflets for a while, and then Mr Fogg takes over, so we wander up to buy an ice cream. It's sunny but not blazing. Perfect really.

'We got the beach sorted,' says Jacob.

'Hmm,' says Eric. 'Just the small matter of the mayor then.'

Which is when the fire brigade appear outside the Royal Hotel and everyone pours out through the doors.

'Awful . . . rodents everywhere . . . even the cereal.'

'Look at my silk pyjamas – ruined . . .'

'And rats in the wiring. It's the last straw. I'm off!'

They trail out, suitcases and dressing gowns in hand, as the firemen trail in.

Eric's cheeks flush red, his forehead remains white and his hair springs up and down. 'Oh dear, what have we done?'

'Don't worry,' I say, feeling 35% sick, and wondering if we haven't done something totally dreadful. 'It'll be fine.'

'What is it?' asks Jacob. 'What's wrong?'

More people leave, and the manager comes out to remonstrate with a large woman who hits him with her wheelie suitcase, and everyone cheers.

'Oh no,' says Eric. 'She should be hitting us.'

'Hmm,' I say – now feeling 55% sick.

'Have you done something wrong, Snot Face?' asks Jacob, a grin spreading across his face.

'Um,' says Eric in reply.

The revolving door at the front of the hotel whizzes into hyper spin and a man in cook's overalls rushes out clutching the scrambled-egg tray – 'Arghghghghgh!' he screams, dropping it in the middle of the road. Even from this distance I can make out a little deckchair snapping and stirring in the egg. 'It's alive! It's alive!' he shouts.

The crowd recoils and a fireman rushes forward with a gigantic hose pouring a huge amount of water in a tiny amount of time. The water ricochets from the pan, spraying anyone anywhere nearby with wet globs of scrambled egg.

'Oh dear,' says Eric again as the mayor

arrives on a bicycle, unslept and unwashed, his eyes wide, shouting, 'Come back, come back. You must come back.'

Half-heartedly I try to convince Eric that it's for the greater good as we turn our backs on the chaos outside the Royal Hotel.

'It means that the hotel won't be bought up and go all horrible,' I say.

'But the poor people,' says Eric. 'How awful to be attacked in your bed by a rampant deckchair.'

Jacob laughs. 'Wish I'd seen it,' he says, picking scrambled egg from his shorts.

'NO, NO and thrice NO!' comes a shout from along the harbour.

It's Marigold, of Marigold Tours.

'NO, I will not sell it to you for almost nothing.' She's shouting at a man in a black suit with a yellow sun hat. 'That is an insult to the years I've spent building up the business. You can take a hike!'

I can't hear what the man says, but Marigold looks thunderous. 'There is nothing wrong with my boat – I have thousands of passengers every year!'

A small crowd gathers to watch.

'I think they've found the other deckchairs,' says Eric. 'Poor Marigold.'

'It's fine,' I say, watching the ship's captain shovelling a dustpan load of deckchairs over the side into the harbour.

'Tom!'

I look round. Albert Fogg is hauling himself up the steps from the beach.

'Here,' I say.

'Tom – have you seen the mayor? It's just that the beach people want to talk to him.' Mr

Fogg looks very excited. 'I think, between you and me, that it might be in the bag.'

But we can't find the mayor. He was last seen outside the Royal Hotel. We go to knock on his front door, but the door's open wide and everything's gone.

'He's done a runner,' says Jacob with great authority.

Which is probably exactly what he has done.

'What?' says Albert Fogg when we tell him. 'He can't have – they can't present the prize without a mayor! Oh no, it's a calamity.' Mr Fogg sinks to the sand, plunging his head between his hands and a long tear escapes from his tiny hidden eyes.

'No,' I say. 'Give us a minute. It's not a calamity, it's an opportunity.'

28

VOTE!

We convince Cheerful Charlie to entertain the judges with a slap-up lunch in the café.

'Just for an hour or two – please? For Mr Fogg?'

'I can't make it last that long – I do fast food.'

'Try doing slow food,' says Eric. 'It's healthier.'

'Right,' I say outside the café, 'we've got to run an election in two hours.'

Jacob blows a bubblegum bubble that pops all over his face. 'Easy-peasy, not,' he says.

'It was going to happen anyway,' I say. 'On Tuesday. We've just got to get the polling booths open and the people into them.'

'Do you think Mr Fogg has a megaphone?' asks Eric.

'You ask, and I'll run and get Mum,' I say.

'What shall I do?' asks Jacob, picking bubblegum from his eyebrow.

I look at him. 'I don't know. Whatever you feel you could do most helpfully.'

Jacob stares at me. Slow tumbleweed thoughts roll across behind his eyes.

'I'll go and buy some sweets,' he says.

'This is all very exciting,' says Mum.

'Yes,' says Eric's dad, who is wearing his best Hawaiian shirt and mismatched lime-green trousers. 'It is.' He doesn't actually look as if it's very exciting. He looks as if he'd rather be digging a deep hole somewhere.

'And,' says Mum, 'you're bound to win, Colin.'

'Am I?' He looks round in astonishment.

'Well, yes,' says Mum. 'I was running against you, and now I'm your vice mayor, and the old mayor has gone. So you're the only candidate.'

'We still have to get enough votes to make it legal though,' I say, repeating something Eric said, which makes me sound wiser than I feel.

'I'll get on the phone to the town clerk,' says Mum. 'Come on, Colin, let's get down to the town hall and get it going. Tom, you and your friends get the voters out.'

I run faster than I can down towards the beach, where Eric's voice is booming from the sand and echoing along the seafront.

'*Ladies, gentlemen and offspring,*' he announces through Mr Fogg's megaphone.

'Bywater-by-Sea may possibly have won the Best Beach award – BUT we cannot claim it without an incumbent mayor so we need your votes – go to the town hall, please, now! Was that all right, Tom?'

He startles the seagulls into flight and makes toddlers cry.

'Yes, fine,' I say, watching the first people leaving their families on the beach to trail up to the town hall. 'Let's try it in the harbour too.'

Dogs bark at us, and a small boy tries to stick an orange in the front of the megaphone as we announce the election in the harbour.

'Could you go and vote please today, if it's not too much trouble, so that we can win the Best Beach contest? That would be really helpful.'

In the centre of town, it's easier to tell each shopkeeper in turn, although this time I have a go on the megaphone – *'Please, everybody, could you go and cast your vote so that we've got a mayor so that we can win the Best Beach contest and make Mr Fogg really happy – did I say please?'* – and shock someone into dropping a tray of coffees.

Lastly we run up to the castle and shout it from the castle battlements but the battery's giving out so it comes out a little mangled:

'Vote now . . . town hall . . . immediately . . . mayor . . . please . . . beach . . . thanks.'

The ladies in the tea shop agree to go and vote in a rota and so within an hour we've covered the whole town.

'I think we'd better go to the town hall now,' says Eric, jamming the megaphone in the back of his shorts and breaking into a lolloping jog.

We race down from the castle and cross back into the harbour, peering in at the door of the Trusty Tramper.

'Oh and I must tell you about the year a hot-air balloon got stuck in the castle – oh how we laughed.' Cheerful Charlie flashes me a desperate smile and points at the three judges, who are yawning and looking at their watches. 'Won't take a moment,' she says.

We charge away from the café and up the hill to the town hall. Eric heaves and puffs behind me as we crash in through the doors.

'Sssshhhh!' says Mum. 'They're counting. It's very exciting.'

'Yes, shhh, Tom,' says Jacob, appearing by my side.

'But you know the result,' I say. 'Eric's dad is the only candidate.'

'Yes, but there's still the thrill of the chase,' she whispers.

'And the result of the count is: Colin Threepwood, 882 votes.' The town clerk beams at Eric's dad, who smiles and looks desperately towards Mum.

'Was that wise?' asks Jacob. 'Shouldn't we have elected someone else – someone not bonkers, someone with more . . . charisma – like me?'

'You have to be over eighteen,' says Eric. 'And Dad isn't bonkers – he's just different.'

'You've got to come with us,' I say, grabbing Eric's dad from Mum and a scary-looking woman with a huge brass necklace that she's trying to put over his head.

'What? Where are we going?' he asks, reaching for Eric's hand.

'Your first official duty,' says Eric. 'Winning the Best Beach contest for Albert Fogg. C'mon, Dad.'

29

Fogg. Frog and a Bucket

We've managed to make Eric's dad look almost normal, arranging him casually against a bollard on the seafront, his Hawaiian shirt blending with the brightly coloured beachgoers, his socks and sandals quickly replaced by bare sandy feet. He doesn't exactly look like someone from Miami, but he looks less like someone from planet Zog than he did ten minutes ago.

'Ah – Mayor Threepwood,' says the pointy woman, wiping a moustache of coffee foam from her top lip. 'How excellent – now we'd like to make a presentation to you and Mr Frog if possible.'

'Fogg,' says Eric.

'Fog?' says the woman.

'Mr Fogg,' says Eric. 'He's called Mr Fogg.'

'Oh,' says the woman. 'What a coincidence – so there's Mr Frog and Mr Fog, how funny – ha, ha, ha.' She laughs hard and high. I do hope she doesn't have any children. No one needs a parent with a laugh like that.

'Er – thank you,' says Eric's dad, holding tight to the bollard. 'I'm sure Albert deserves it.'

The woman looks confused. 'Albert?'

'Mr Frog,' I say quickly.

Jacob brings Mr Fogg up the steps and they stand solidly, waiting.

'So – we'd like to present you, Mr Fog and

Mr Frog, with this, the Best Beach award golden bucket and spade – hurrah! Ha, ha, ha.' She holds the bucket out towards Eric's dad.

Mr Fogg grabs it and gazes at it. It looks suspiciously like a plastic bucket and spade sprayed with gold spray paint but from the look on Mr Fogg's face he's seeing real twenty-four-carat gold. 'Ah,' he says. 'Ah. That's lovely that is. Ah . . .'

'Good,' says Eric's dad, curling his toes into the sand. 'Good.'

'Is that it?' says Jacob. 'Is that what all the fuss has been about?'

The following morning, we sit on the sea wall, our legs dangling over the front. It's a beautiful late spring day, with sunlight dipping on and off the water, seagulls wheeling over our heads and a gentle breeze playing over our toes.

It would all be perfect except Mum and Dad are with us, beaming and sharing out slightly stale chocolate that I recognise from Grandma's larder.

'It seems,' says Mum, handing me a square of whitish chocolate, 'that the hotel deal broke down. Something to do with mice.'

I go bright red. 'Oh!' I say.

'Goodness,' says Eric, turning redder than I've ever seen him. 'Mice, did you say? We wouldn't know anything about that – would we, Tom?'

I kick Eric. Sometimes you have to kick nice people just to stop them digging holes for themselves.

Mum doesn't appear to notice. 'And without the mayor to hold the negotiations together,

Gogleplex walked away from the table, and so did the burger chain and the sofa people. They've all gone as fast as they arrived.'

'Were they all sitting at one table?' asks Jacob.

'It's a figure of speech,' says Mum, just as Eric opens his mouth to say the same thing.

'So,' I say, 'no multi-million-pound company is going to come to Bywater-by-Sea? Not even the sofas?'

'Seems not,' says Mum. 'I mean, in one way it's marvellous of course, but in another it's a bit of a tragedy. Without the money they would have brought – the town's in a pretty poor way.'

'Mr Fogg did say something about that – but how come?' asks Eric.

'The mayor. He's been squandering the town's money right, left and centre – big lunches, consultants, five-year plans, all that sort of thing. It's awful. It really is just as well that we won the Best Beach contest – at least it'll bring in the holidaymakers.'

'And at least Mr Fogg is happy,' I say. 'He won the competition; he's got the bucket and spade.'

'But that's exactly the point. He's retired – as of tomorrow – off to run a web-design business, so the only thing that makes any money is likely to stop until we can find some poor mug prepared to lug all those chairs in and out every day.'

'I've been thinking,' says Dad.

We turn to look at him.

'I'm wondering if I'm cut out for school work – I mean, look at this.' He waves airily over the beach and the sea. 'I mean, who'd not want to be here all the time – renting out the chairs, fixing the pedalos – a simple life, but a happy one.'

'Are you saying you'd like to take on Albert Fogg's job?' says Mum.

After a long pause, Dad says, 'Yes.'

30

Baby Otter Loses his Hair

Which leaves Tilly.

And twelve tiny, but slowly growing, vicious deckchairs.

And one parasol.

Oh and a hole in the rock.

The rock is comparatively simple. Grandma comes with us to have a look.

'Ooh my,' she says. 'It must go all the way to the castle. So you think it's the meteorite dust mixed with the water?' she asks Eric.

He nods. 'Yes, and it's a steady flow, there must be water trickling through somewhere. If we drain it into the sea then it would dissolve harmlessly.'

Jacob stares at the crack. 'Couldn't I just melt the rock until it seals up?'

We all stare at him.

'That's almost a genius suggestion,' says Eric. 'Except the water needs to come out somewhere.'

'We could drill another hole,' says Jacob, 'somewhere else in the rock, just not in the cave.'

'O – K,' I say. 'How? Where?'

Jacob doesn't answer, just swaggers down the beach and stops under the pier where the sea comes in closer to the shore.

He turns to Eric. 'Ready, tap-fingered Snot Face?'

'S'pect so.' Eric looks bewildered.

Jacob fires a fireball at the rock, smashing

it and heating it up until it smokes.

Eric sprays it. For a second the rock steams and then, shocked by the extreme temperatures, crumbles.

Again, Jacob fires sheets of flame.

Again, Eric shoots water.

This time, a tiny crack becomes a fissure, and quickly the fissure becomes a canyon, and before very long water begins to dribble from the hole, seeping into the sand and down to the sea.

'Wow, Jacob,' says Eric. 'Thermal shock – excellent.'

'Wow indeed,' says Grandma.

So that's one problem solved.

Then there are the remaining deckchairs.

'You can't leave them running about, Tom, you do know that, don't you?' says Grandma. 'You boys will have to round them up.'

We find them roosting in the bird reserve. A line of little chairs and a single parasol snapping and chattering alongside the limpets.

'Now what?' says Jacob.

'We can try to steam-clean them again,' I say.

'Or just burn them,' says Jacob, sparks leaping from his fingers.

But perhaps they hear us, or perhaps they're really turning into seabirds, because the moment we approach all twelve dive from their perch into the sea and swim off, leaving the parasol, which twirls once, puts itself up and floats onto the water before drifting seawards, squeaking and rustling in search of its friends.

'What will happen to them?' I ask, scratching my head.

'Ultimately they'll become waterlogged,' says Eric.

'And then sink?' asks Jacob.

'Or set up a colony somewhere,' says Eric.

I gaze at the beach furniture until I can't be sure if they're what I'm seeing or simply part of the horizon.

'Suppose they wash up in France and attack people there?' I say.

'Not our problem,' says Jacob.

'So you haven't really learned anything about empathy then?' says Eric.

'What?' says Jacob.

'Don't worry,' says Eric. 'I don't think I can be bothered to explain.'

'Of course I'm pleased that Dad's stopped coming to school!' shouts Tilly, dropping baby otter into a pan of boiling water.

'Why are you doing that?' asks Eric, reaching for a spoon and leaning over the pan.

'He's been bad,' she says, brushing Eric away. 'And I want him to beg for mercy.'

'But he's plastic,' I reply. The fake fur curls away from baby otter's nose revealing the brown plastic underneath.

'Exactly,' she replies. 'He's altogether unresponsive.' She barely pauses for breath. 'But I'm furious that Dad's going to be on the beach all day – imagine – every single person at school will see him forever and ever selling those deckchairs and pedalos and –' she pauses for a long dramatic sigh – 'it'll be terrible – no one will ever talk to me again – I'll be sent to Coventry, ostracised, given the cold shoulder – never again invited to anyone's birthday party, never again taken home after school, never again voted for in the best handwriting competition, never again sing the solo, never again picked to be teacher's helper – it'll be –' she drags in a breath – 'terrible.'

Jacob, who has so far stayed silent, gazes at Tilly, his mouth wide. 'Awesome,' he says. 'That was utterly awesome.'

'It was rather good, wasn't it?' says Tilly, smiling, and poking at baby otter who is now almost completely bald.

We all stare at the brown plastic thing bobbing in the boiling water.

'It won't be that bad, Tilly,' I say. 'Over time they'll forget that he's our dad – and it's so much better than having him on the bus. And he won't be out and about in the winter. He'll be painting deckchairs or whatever it is that Mr Fogg did in the winter. And Mum's not going to be mayor. She's just going to be Eric's dad's right-hand man, so people won't really know she's there either.'

Tilly stops prodding baby otter and takes the pan from the stove. She turns to look at me, folding her arms and relaxing her shoulders. She scrapes the point of her toe in a semi-circle, glances out of the window and then back at me. 'I suppose you're right. I'm overreacting, and I realise that it's not just me suffering with all this – it's you too, Tom.' She smiles at me. A genuine, warm, loving, sisterly smile.

We stare at her, open-mouthed.

31
Empathy?

I'm feeling confused.

Tilly has never ever shown me the slightest bit of warmth, love or kindness her entire life. Except when she wants something and then she shows me something vaguely like, but not at all exactly the same as, kindness. But this time I can't work out what she wants.

The school's empathy drive has either worked, she's growing up, or she's entered a new phase of her acting career and is taking on an extra persona. It's disturbing.

Later on, when Mum's got the town accounts laid out all over the kitchen table and she and Grandma are going through them looking for ways to make or save money, Tilly tiptoes past, helps herself to a yoghurt and tiptoes back.

She doesn't disturb them. She doesn't say 'Look at me!' She doesn't do anything at all.

When Dad's trying on a new version of Albert Fogg's ancient yellow waterproof, Tilly doesn't shout at him. She looks momentarily excessively tragic before helping him to pull up the sleeve.

I so don't get it.

Dad does his first day of work on the beach. Tilly actually offers to take him a sandwich.

I struggle with Miss Mawes's new art assignment – a copy of the *Mona Lisa* in rice. I'm feeling 99% lousy about it. Tilly comes past, lays a reassuring hand on my shoulder and says: 'Don't worry, Tom, she'll soon realise you're hopeless at art.' I glance up and see that she doesn't even mean it in a horrible way.

My mental jaw drops even further.

Mum spends all day in the office at the town hall sifting through receipts, and when she gets home Tilly offers her a cup of tea.

Mum nearly falls off her chair. 'Well – I suppose, yes. I would like a cup.'

Tilly presents her with tea and doesn't even wait for Mum to say thank you.

'Is she ill?' asks Jacob.

I shake my head. 'I think she's genuinely changed,' I say.

'Maybe she has,' says Eric. 'Although . . .'

But I suppose the proof comes a few days later when my head itches so badly that I run screaming downstairs to Mum.

She peers into my hair. 'Oh dear – yes – head lice.'

I sit on the stool of shame while Mum pours conditioner on my head and drags the comb through.

'Ow!' I squeak.

'Sorry,' says Mum. 'But it's bound to hurt.'

Tilly throws open the kitchen door, and although for a millisecond I'm pretty sure I spy a smug face, she stops, gazes towards me and wrestles with her features until something sympathetic surfaces. 'Oh, Tom – did I give you nits? I'm so sorry.'

Mum drops the comb. I yank my head round.

'Really?' says Mum.

'I am,' says Tilly. 'They're awful – and the combing can be really painful.'

Grandma comes in from the garden, and

pulls off her wellingtons. 'Oh dear – another one?' she says.

'Yes, poor Tom,' says Tilly. 'And it's all my fault. I sort of gave them to him on purpose. I was really cross that morning when you'd all been out all night.'

'Out all night?' asks Mum.

'I'll explain later,' says Grandma hastily.

'So I went to Tom's bedroom and laid my hair on the pillow right next to him. I knew I still had head lice and . . .' She looks at me, her eyes big and round and almost tearful. 'I'm really sorry. It's a terribly selfish thing to have done.'

Grandma raises her eyebrows. 'Goodness. Anyway, I've just heard from Albert Fogg – who is, incidentally, loving his retirement – apparently he's already got 324 subscribers, whatever that means.' Grandma struggles to pull up her sock. 'Although he also said that Mrs Santos had a nasty moment when she went to change the flowers at the old lock-up.' Grandma looks up and stares hard at me.

I redden under the conditioner.

'What happened?' asks Mum.

'Some deckchairs fell on her – she broke a vase apparently,' says Grandma. 'Quite a hoo-ha. She got in quite a panic, had to call the fire brigade.'

'Oh no,' I say. 'How dreadful.'

There's a squeak from the other side of the room. I look round to Tilly, who is holding her hand over her mouth, suppressing a squall of giggles. I know what she's thinking – she's thinking of round little Mrs Santos having to be rescued from under a pile of snapping deckchairs.

It might be funny, but I still stare at her.

We all stare.

She pulls her face straight, swallows and purses her lips. Only the tears in her eyes give her away. 'Oh, poor Mrs Santos, how dreadful for her – what a shock. Poor thing, I do hope she's recovered.'

It's not really empathy, but we're getting there.

 **SMALL TOWN, BIG MAGIC ...**

Have you read them all yet?

Also by Fleur Hitchcock:

Find out more at:

www.piccadillypress.co.uk

Thank you for choosing a Piccadilly Press book.

If you would like to know more about our authors, our books or if you'd just like to know what we're up to, you can find us online.

www.piccadillypress.co.uk

You can also find us on:

We hope to see you soon!